JUDAS
IN JERUSALEM

◦ *a novel* ◦

JOSEPH LEWIS HEIL

Lake Lore Press

Published by

Lake Lore Press

Second softcover, paper edition published by Lake Lore Press, December, 2018.

Second Kindle e-book edition published by Joseph Lewis Heil, December, 2018.

ISBN-13: 978-0-69218-589-6

Cover design by Dionisio C. Manalo Jr. aka "Evocative" at www.99designs.com

Interior layout by Gary A. Rosenberg: www.garyarosenberg.com

Image of Palestine at the Time of Jesus from Bible History Online.

CONTENTS

Acknowledgments   vii

Author's Note   ix

Map of Palestine at the Time of Jesus   xi

Prologue ~ *In the hill country.*   1

Chapter 1 ~ *A desert encounter.*   7

Chapter 2 ~ *Jesus assigns his purse.*   15

Chapter 3 ~ *An arrest at the Jordan.*   19

Chapter 4 ~ *John, the baptizer, imprisoned.*   25

Chapter 5 ~ *Jesus & Judas in Ephraim.*   29

Chapter 6 ~ *The death of John, the baptizer.*   33

Chapter 7 ~ *To Jerusalem.*   39

Chapter 8 ~ *Two women to Jerusalem.*   43

Chapter 9 ~ *A Jerusalem dinner party.*   51

Chapter 10 ~ *The return to Bethany.*   59

Chapter 11 ~ *Judas at the house of Lazarus.*   63

Chapter 12 ~ *Judas visits Simon, a merchant.*   67

Chapter 13 ~ *Martha's opinions.*   73

Chapter 14 ~ *A plan and a price.*   75

Chapter 15 ~ *An enjoyable afternoon.*   79

Chapter 16 ~ *The Alley of Red Lanterns.*   83

Chapter 17 ~ *A walk from Jericho to Bethany.*   91

Chapter 18 ~ *Pontius Pilate enters Jerusalem.*   99

Chapter 19 ~ *A trap is set.*   107

Chapter 20 ~ *An unexpected visit.*   119

Chapter 21 ~ *Judas's assignment.*   123

Chapter 22 ~ *Simon's bewilderment.*   127

Chapter 23 ~ *A fateful kiss.*   137

Chapter 24 ~ *The road to Jerusalem.*   141

Chapter 25 ~ *Dream and reality.*   147

Chapter 26 ~ *The death of Judas.*   155

Epilogue ~ *A final prophecy.*   165

Ad Majorem Dei Gloriam

&

To my family and many friends.

*The argument favoring the beauty of virtue
cannot be won without revealing
the ugliness of vice.*

—JLH

ACKNOWLEDGMENTS

Early drafts of the manuscript were read by my wife, Ursula, my children, Joseph Jr., Jennifer, Christine, and Jeffrey, my brother, John N. Heil, a published author at https://www.goodreads.com/author/show/691722.John_N_Heil, my son-in-law, James Prebil, and many friends including Ray Laub, Mary White, Lou Patscot, Sonja Immekus, Richard Duveneck, Bill McCarty, and Christine Frymark All provided valuable feedback and helpful criticism.

Special thanks to my wife who is my in-home, natural born editor. Intuitively, and with great taste, she knows what's good and what isn't, what works and what doesn't.

Also, special thanks to my *literary* friends, both fine writers: Andrew Clarke at http://www.andrewclarkestories.com and John Greenya, a Washington-based reviewer for local and national publications and author of twenty-four books including his most recent biography of Associate Justice Neil Gorsuch. Read about John at http://www.fauquiernow.com/

AUTHOR'S NOTE

For two millennia, Christian theology has recognized the duality of the nature of Jesus Christ as both fully human and fully divine.

The four evangelists, Matthew, Mark, Luke, and John, chronicled the life of Jesus with emphasis on his divinity.

Judas In Jerusalem, as fiction, alludes only to the human nature of Jesus in interactions with twelve close friends (the apostles), and the people of Palestine.

However, the primary focus of the novel examines the human nature of Judas Iscariot, historically cast as the so-called "betrayer" of Jesus. The gospel writers reveal little about Judas except that he was a thief, keeper of the purse for Jesus, and, ultimately, Jesus' betrayer. Driven by fear and greed, Judas identified Jesus, which led to his arrest and subsequent fateful interrogation by the Sanhedrin, the governing body of the ancient Jewish religion.

This novel imagines Judas's critical four days that preceded his betrayal of Jesus and our Lord's death by crucifixion.

PALESTINE AT THE TIME OF JESUS

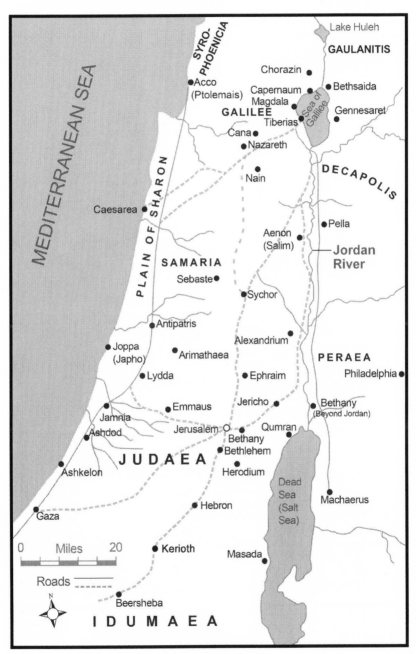

PROLOGUE

In the hill country.

At the coming of spring's first prophetic winds, a young Galilean woman, Mary of Nazareth, and her only son began their yearly journey to visit an elderly cousin in the distant hill country near Jerusalem. Elizabeth and her son lived in the Judean village of En Kerem.

Over a decade earlier when pregnant, Mary came to this house of Zachariah. Greeting her then, Elizabeth exclaimed that the child within her womb leapt with joy. Now those sons of Elizabeth and Mary, John and Jesus, were bound like brothers.

In clear, middle eastern air the boys ran and raced, wrestled each other, and climbed rugged Sycamores that marked the rolling hills. When their energy was gone, they sprawled in cool, willowy meadows to gaze at white cumulus floating overhead in a cobalt sky. Evenings, after supper, they spread blankets on the dewy grass, all the while studying the black dome above, girdled by a long, bright belt of milky stardust. Night after night, they noticed some star positions had changed, offering an inscrutable mystery. They would stare and wonder and talk of every-thing they knew and dreamed until their mothers called them in.

Mary asked, "My goodness, what do you boys all talk about?"

"What do any thirteen year old boys talk about?" Elizabeth answered.

At the morning meal, John told of seeing stars with blazing speed streak in silence across the sky. Both mothers replied they, too, had seen such wondrous things, although they had no idea what they could possibly be or might mean.

More concerned about practical matters, Mary asked, "John, what do you want to do when you grow up?"

"I don't know."

"Jesus is learning to be a carpenter, like his father. You could come and stay with us awhile and begin to learn the carpenter's trade. Joseph would be happy to teach you."

"I don't want to be a carpenter," John said.

"Well you have to do something worthwhile," Elizabeth said. "Once you've grown up, you can't run around all day and gaze at stars half the night."

"I like carpentry," Jesus said. "I like building things, and I like working with my father. We build tables, chairs, beds, things people use . . . sometimes we even build a roof."

"I don't want to be a carpenter," John repeated.

Jesus stood next to John and said, "Feel my muscle," offering his flexed bicep right in John's face. "My father taught me to hew and shape logs into posts and beams. They're heavy. Lifting makes me strong."

John pushed Jesus away. "I'm not interested in your muscles or being a carpenter."

"Jesus helps his father now with every job he has. Joseph told me he gets so much more done in a day because of Jesus' help."

"Why that's wonderful," Elizabeth said. "See, John, your cousin is working like a grown man."

John said nothing, stood, and went outside. Jesus followed.

"I must tell you, Mary, I worry about John. It's wonderful when Jesus visits, but John doesn't play like that with boys in our village, at least not as much as I think he should. He strikes me as being too solitary, too alone . . . unsociable."

"He seems perfectly normal to me."

"After Zachariah died I noticed a change in John. He grew more into himself, more reclusive."

"Losing his father wasn't easy. . . ."

"The problem was his father was more like a grandfather. I'm even beginning to feel more like a grandmother. We were too old to have a child."

"It was God's will," Mary said. "You know that because of the sign."

Zachariah had been a priest at Herod's Temple in Jerusalem. After he finally drew the lot to offer prayers at the sacred altar, he was struck mute for doubting God that Elizabeth would still conceive, well aware she was too old to bear a child. Nevertheless, she did conceive. At the baby's circumcision and naming, Zachariah wrote on a tablet that the boy must be called John, which means *God is gracious.* Immediately Zachariah's voice was restored.

"Yes, Mary, I know, but it was difficult for John losing his father. He taught him to read and love the scriptures, indeed to love God."

"How wonderful. . . ."

"Well, not entirely: it was Zachariah who encouraged John to star gaze, something they did together, and something he does almost every night now, not just when Jesus is here. Unfortunately, Zachariah didn't teach him a useful trade. Oh, how I wish John wanted to be a carpenter. It would so ease my worrying."

"You shouldn't worry. You must trust God. His will be done, not ours. Besides, I see John as a very normal thirteen year old."

"Is it normal for a boy his age to sit up in a tree half the day—I mean, all by himself?"

Before Mary could answer, both boys came back in.

Not wanting to reveal what they had been discussing, Elizabeth asked, "Tell me, Jesus, do you study scripture?"

Abruptly, Mary answered. "Of course he does. When we were in Jerusalem last year, presenting Jesus in the Temple, he began to discuss scripture with many scribes and scholars. They were amazed at his knowledge and understanding."

John said, "I read scripture. I like it."

"So what would you like to be when you grow up?" Mary asked again.

John thought for a moment. "Maybe a priest, like my father, except I don't like Jerusalem—too many animals, too stinky, too many people."

"The stipend is way too small," Elizabeth said. "You still have to master a trade if you want to eat. You should think about that instead of daydreaming."

Surprising everyone, Jesus said, "I like helping my father, but I don't intend to be a carpenter when I grow up. Why should John?"

John laughed. "That's how I feel. I don't know what I want, but I don't want a trade."

Both boys laughed, annoying their mothers.

"Jesus," Mary reprimanded, "you enjoy carpentry; you told me so many times. Since when don't you want to be a carpenter? You're becoming one. That's what you will be, just like your father."

"No, Mother," Jesus said, "I'm not sure what I'm supposed to do with my life, but it's not carpentry. I'm certain of that."

"I'm not sure what I'm supposed to do either," John said.

Exasperated, Elizabeth said, "You boys need to grow up, especially you, John."

"We will," Jesus said. "In good time, we will."

CHAPTER I

A desert encounter.

The Sun at its zenith scorched the desert floor. Heated, layered air shimmered above the baking sand. In this Judean wilderness west of the Dead Sea, John, cousin of Jesus, lived in a crude camp pitched against a high, sheltering ridge. Now, shielding his eyes while gazing toward the distant south, John saw a cloaked and hooded man no more than fifty paces from his camp. The man staggered, then fell.

John ran to him, wondering if the man had died.

A twitching arm revealed he had not.

John carried the unconscious man to his camp, laying him on a mat beneath the tent roof. John palmed the bearded face's burning brow; he grasped the wayfarer's thin arms and legs.

For three days John cared for the emaciated man who slipped in and out of consciousness until his fever finally broke.

"Friend, who are you?" John asked. "What's your name?"

"Water . . . more water. . . ."

The man drank then slumped back onto the mat.

Again John asked, "What's your name?"

"My name is Judas."

After eating several times, Judas slowly regained his strength. Next day, he rose and walked about. That evening, their last together, they ate and conversed.

"Where do you come from, Judas?"

"I grew up in Kerioth, a town in southern Judea."

"So, you are a man from Kerioth, or, as the Greeks would say, Judas Iscariot."

"I wouldn't know that. I don't know Greek."

"Why did you leave Kerioth?"

"I left because my father was dead, and my mother no longer wanted me."

"Why was that?"

Judas paused, uncomfortable with the question. John, curious to know, urged him to answer. A cooling, desert breeze wafted through the camp. "Tell me about yourself, Judas."

After several moments, he said, "We were poor. Our house was a shack. My clothes were shabbier than other boy's. People didn't think much of us, and girls made fun of me. Oftentimes my father got drunk. He didn't work, not like other men. My mother took in laundry to get by.

"At night my father came home late, reeking of wine. My mother hated it. She called him ugly names; then he'd beat her. When I was little I couldn't protect, but when I got older I tried. Then he'd beat me. We ran from the house. We'd wait a long while, hoping he'd fall asleep. That's usually what happened."

"That's terrible, Judas. That's no way for a family to live."

"No, but then something wonderful happened."

"What?" John asked.

"My father died. People said too much wine poisoned his blood. We believed it."

"Were your lives better then?"

"Yes . . . until my mother took in another man."

"Did he take her as his wife?"

Judas laughed contemptuously. "He took her as his whore."

"You shouldn't say that about your mother."

"Why not? It's true. I hated her for it."

"That's sad. You and your mother are to be pitied."

"I don't want pity. She didn't love me, at least not as much as that guy."

"What was he like—not a drunkard, I hope?"

"No, but after a few weeks, he turned on me. At first it was okay, but then, when my mother wasn't there, he got mean. My father wasn't mean, except when he got drunk, but even then it was different. This man was cruel; slapped my head, told me I was stupid, told me he didn't want me in the house. He even claimed my mother didn't want me when I was born. Believe me, I grew to hate him very quickly."

"Was he the reason you left Kerioth?"

"One of them. Eventually, he convinced my mother I had to leave, said I was too old and our shack too small for two grown men. I was only fifteen. He said he'd only support her. She told me I had to go, so I left."

"How did you live?"

"I worked planting and harvesting. I fed goats and oxen and shoveled dung. Often I had to beg." Pain tainted Judas's voice. "For God's sake, I was always hungry; I had no decent place to sleep. I was dirty, my clothes were filthy rags. Everybody shunned me."

John shook his head. "Terrible, just terrible."

Judas closed his eyes. A deep sadness marked his face. Shame at what he was about to reveal dwelt in his heart.

"Boys and even some townspeople called me *Stupid Judas*. I hated it. That's why I left."

"Why did they call you that?"

"Because I can't read or write. My parents didn't take me to synagogue; I never had a teacher. Most Jews in Kerioth took their children, but my parents were too stupid, too poor. The little money we had, my father wasted on wine. He couldn't read either."

Both men fell silent. John, troubled by the wretchedness of Judas's early life, stood and went outside. The desert air was pleasant under a sky white with stars.

Coming back into the dimly lit tent, John noticed Judas's eyes scanning John's meager possessions. He asked Judas what he was looking for.

"Nothing—you have so little," Judas said.

Then John asked where Judas was headed when he rescued him from a certain desert death.

"I'm on my way to Jerusalem. I'll fare better there."

"A young man who can't read will not meet with any success in Jerusalem. It's a very learned city. What skills do you have?"

"I'm a beggar. I have no skills." Judas did not want to reveal any more about himself, especially his most proficient skill, so he asked, "Can I stay here, at least for a while?"

"No," John answered. "I prefer to be alone."

"Why? Why would you want to live like that?" Judas knew how hard it was.

"Because in this desert silence, and my solitude, I am better able to hear the voice of God."

Amazed, but skeptical, Judas asked, "Does he really speak to you?"

"Yes, I believe he does."

"What does he say?"

"He urges me to warn people to repent their sins and, if they do, I am to baptize them."

"What do you mean . . . baptize?"

"Crowds gather at the Jordan. I baptize those who truly

repent. To baptize means to immerse in water, thus to purify that which sin has soiled. It's an action that affirms repentance and symbolizes cleanliness."

Judas said, "I wouldn't do that, and besides, I have no sins."

"We all have sinned, Judas, even you, though you might not realize it."

Judas felt uneasy with John's remarks. The prospect of being fully immersed, of actually being placed underwater, frightened him. And he was sure he hadn't committed serious sin, though oftentimes he had to steal to eat. But, in his mind, that was no sin at all, because he knew God wouldn't want him to die of mere hunger. And, to his self-proclaimed credit, he never stole from the poor, though they really had nothing worth stealing.

He had checked John's things, utensils and such, but saw nothing of any use to himself save, perhaps, one. Judas felt no strong need to steal from the baptizer who generously offered meals of bread, wild honey, and fruit. Yet, as always was the case, if an opportunity came, temptation would invade his heart. And after he fell, it was his poverty that always justified the sin.

John began again. "I have an idea, Judas. My cousin is a teacher who travels throughout Galilee and Judea with a band of followers. Before you go to Jerusalem, seek him out. He won't be difficult to find, just ask anyone you come across. His name is Jesus, from the town of Nazareth.

Most people in Galilee have heard of him; he's a teacher of great knowledge and wisdom. I believe Jesus would be willing to teach you to read, especially if you tell him I sent you for that reason. Perhaps, Judas, you can even join Jesus' followers."

John's suggestion immediately interested Judas. "I'm a good counter. I can summate in my head."

"Then perhaps my cousin will have need for you, as he and his friends have to eat, find shelter, and replace worn out clothes and sandals. So, if you can help him collect funds, Jesus might be happy to have you and teach you as well."

With that proposal, Judas experienced something he hadn't felt in his young life: a simple hope to actually learn and do something worthwhile. "Yes, I'll seek your cousin." Then after a pause, "Can I sleep here tonight? I promise I'll leave in the morning."

"Yes, but only tonight. Tomorrow, after we break our fast, you must leave."

Judas Iscariot fell asleep contentedly, something he hadn't experienced since his earliest childhood.

In the morning, John wished Judas peace and good luck and bid him farewell.

After Judas was out of sight, John prepared to go to the Jordan for water. He hung his water bags from nails in a tent post. He had six including a fine, leather bag that an admirer whom he baptized had given him. But now the bag was not at its appointed nail. In its place was a shabby, tattered bag.

"Ah," John sighed. To the desert wind he said aloud, "As I suspected, Judas Iscariot, you are a thief."

CHAPTER 2

Jesus assigns his purse.

Within weeks after leaving John, Judas encountered Jesus and his followers on the road north of Jericho. When Judas explained to Jesus it was his cousin who urged Judas to seek him, Jesus exclaimed his delight, but hid his puzzlement. *Why would it be John?* he wondered.

"How is my cousin? Is he still baptizing in the Jordan?"

"Yes, he told me he does that. I didn't know what baptizing was until he explained it."

"John baptized me several years ago. We'll have to visit John and let him baptize you and some of the others."

Jesus' suggestion troubled Judas. He did not want to encounter John again, and he certainly didn't want to be immersed in a river. Several men stepped away leaving Judas alone with Jesus.

Studying Judas's expression, Jesus asked, "How did you happen to find my cousin?"

"I was headed toward Jerusalem when I stumbled across his camp. I stayed with him several days."

"Hmm, that surprises me," Jesus said. "John prefers to be alone. That's why he lives in the desert."

Judas did not respond.

Jesus asked, "Is there something else you wish to say?"

Again it was difficult for Judas to reveal his inability to read and write, but he did so, adding that John suggested Jesus might be willing to teach him.

"What can you do, Judas, I mean to help my friends and me?"

"I have a knack for handling money," he said, "begging for it, if necessary. I can add, and I can bargain to get things at friendly prices."

Jesus turned and called, "Matthew, come here!"

Matthew had been a tax collector before becoming a follower of Jesus; as such he was skilled at handling money.

Jesus said, "He keeps our purse, but doesn't want that responsibility anymore."

"I'll do it," Judas said, eagerly.

Matthew reached into the deep pocket of his cloak, withdrew a nearly empty money sack and handed it to Judas. "Henceforth, friend, you can be responsible for gathering enough to keep all of us reasonably well-fed, well-clothed and, occasionally, sheltered. There will be thirteen if you join us. We all have hearty appetites—I presume you do, too—but we're not nearly as concerned with the appearance of our garments." He looked Judas up and down. "You, obviously, are not so concerned either."

"I could use some new clothes," Judas admitted. He raised his robe, revealing worn sandals.

"We'll get you some," Jesus said. "Sandals, too."

Matthew said, "You have to be persuasive and, now and then, a good beggar to collect what we need. You have to be persistent, and you have to get used to hearing people say no."

"How do you do it?" Judas asked.

"When Jesus is teaching, I move through the crowd whispering to everyone if they'd be so kind to give a few denarii to help Jesus' ministry. If rich people are there, and they usually are, I ask them for a shekel or two. You can always spot rich people by their clothes and manner. They'll stand apart, or to one side. They want to hear Jesus, but they don't want to mingle with the poor.

"When Jesus finishes teaching, the crowd is enthusiastic, uplifted, and more inclined to give. That's when you have to move quickly, first to the rich and then those nearest Jesus. By then, people will be more apt to give so don't be afraid to ask. And don't be afraid to ask the rich for Roman silver even if they gave you something already. Persistence is key."

"If you believe you can handle it," Jesus said, "then you're welcome to travel with us. If you're successful you will earn our gratitude. If not, you'll have to surrender the purse."

"I'd like to try," Judas said. With his secret skill, he was sure he could gain enough to keep everyone in Jesus' band content. He even imagined there'd be a few extra coins to stash away for himself.

"Well then, I'll give you the opportunity," Jesus said. "I'll also be happy to teach you to read. I'm not exactly a school teacher, but I'm sure I'll have you reading in no time."

"And writing," Judas said. "Someday I hope to go to Jerusalem and find work there."

"Yes, of course. They go together. You speak like there's ambition in your heart."

"There is," Judas replied.

"That's good, as long as your ambition doesn't change your soul."

"What do you mean?"

"You are made in the image and likeness of God, Judas. Don't ever let your ambition or any person or thing make you forget that."

"I won't."

"And soon enough we'll all turn our faces toward Jerusalem, but not before I begin to teach you to read and write."

"That will be good," Judas said.

Jesus turned to walk away, but then turned back. "That's a fine water bag you have. Where'd you get it?"

"Your cousin gave it to me."

CHAPTER 3

An arrest at the Jordan.

With time, Judas Iscariot proved a competent keeper of the purse. He made sure it always held enough for food and, when needed, funds for a new cloak or sandals. Occasionally, he provided all of them the rare pleasure of dining and sleeping at an inn. Then Judas was well praised, praise he relished.

Jesus was pleased, while Matthew welcomed relief from a job he no longer wanted. He admitted he never worked with the same, quiet determination Judas displayed, nor the skill. Other men, however, took Judas's competence more for granted, not really acknowledging that Judas had sole responsibility for collecting sufficient money to satisfy every man's desire to be well-fed and reasonably well-clothed. It was thoughtless of them, for Judas had to do it day after day, week after week, without reprieve. Those others, older and having been with Jesus much longer, were too busy conversing with him, and sometimes arguing among themselves, to notice that Judas was always, necessarily so, working for their benefit.

Actually, that Judas did the job without bringing much attention to himself was his intention. He liked keeping the purse and its contents to himself. It gave him feelings of power and control. Oftentimes, when Jesus sent two or three of his friends ahead to announce to a town his coming, it was Judas, alone, who had to beg from those townspeople and buy from their merchants.

When Jesus taught, Judas moved through the crowd with sly resolve. He was persistent and unafraid to ask any man to give generously. Because he was so intent upon collecting money, he often failed to listen to the fullness of Jesus' teachings. But afterward, he did listen to the conversations of the eleven discussing what Jesus had taught, so he was learning some, if not all, of their Master's teachings.

Judas, actually, was more interested in Jesus as his teacher in the arts of reading and writing. Here, too, Judas proved himself a diligent worker. Within several weeks he had learned to read, and, after that, took earnestly to master the art of writing.

"You learn quickly," Jesus said. "That others once called you stupid was cruel. You were not stupid as a boy, just as you are not stupid as a man. You were uneducated through no fault of your own. Now that you can read, you can progress in your education by your own means, efforts, and desires."

"I intend to," Judas replied.

"Now show me the purse," Jesus said.

There wasn't much in it: a few denarii, no shekels. Jesus took the coins and handed the bag back to Judas.

"What are you doing?" Judas asked.

"Look," Jesus said, pointing at beggars along the road-side. He walked toward them and gave the coins away. Two old women kissed his hands.

"Why must he do that?" Judas asked Matthew who had drawn near.

"Never question the Master."

"I haven't a single denarii to buy bread. Of course now he expects I should go begging again. Who should I beg from—those old hags? They have more money than we do. I get money; he gives it away. That's ridiculous. Why should I work at all?"

"Judas, keep those thoughts to yourself. Do your job. If we have no money then we don't eat. Jesus understands. Many a night before you joined us, we slept with empty bellies."

"It's stupid," Judas persisted. "He expects me to provide for everyone, then he gives away the little in my purse."

"Don't complain," Matthew said. "Besides, it's not your purse."

Jesus and the twelve were heading through the south of Samaria toward Jerusalem, but when they entered

Judea, Jesus turned his face toward Jericho instead. "We'll find my cousin now, so he can baptize those of you who need it."

Judas was deeply disappointed; he yearned to get to Jerusalem, as he had never been to the great city. He wanted to see Jerusalem long before he encountered John in the desert. Judas had no desire to be baptized, and certainly no desire to meet John again. He knew John would reveal how he had cared for Judas for three days, and also how Judas stole John's finest water bag. That, Judas was sure, would not merely harm Judas's friendship with Jesus, but would more likely end it. Plus, his aversion to being fully immersed into the flowing Jordan intensified into fear. The baptizer's activity seemed foolish to Judas unless, he thought, *penitents were merely desirous of a quick bath*. Thus, out of a protective necessity, Judas began to devise ways to avoid John.

After Jesus and the twelve passed through Jericho and approached the Jordan, they met streams of travelers heading in the other direction. Who first learned the stunning news was unclear, but soon all thirteen knew. They beseeched men and women on the road to reveal everything they could. A young Samaritan man was stopped by Jesus. The twelve circled the two to hear all the Samaritan had to tell.

"Yesterday at sundown, King Herod's soldiers came

and arrested the baptizer. Most of the people who had been baptized had left or were leaving. There weren't enough men to save John."

"What charges were brought against him?" Jesus asked.

"I don't know. I came today with many others. We hoped John would appear, but he never did. A messenger from Herod Antipas came on horseback and told the crowd John was arrested and never again would baptize in the Jordan. He told everyone to go home and tell others about John's fate. Someone asked where John was being held. The messenger said at Herod's palace at Machaerus, far to the south. Then he left."

Jesus said, "So now my dear cousin is imprisoned in the dungeon of an evil king."

Peter, one of the twelve, said, "We should go there, demand his release."

"No," Jesus said. "John is a holy man. God will protect him, unless Herod has evil intentions. Against such evil no man is safe, nor could any man dissuade."

Judas listened to it all. While he couldn't imagine or understand why John, a simple, good man, would be arrested, he was relieved, because now he'd probably never encounter John again. *Hopefully, by the time he gets out of prison,* Judas thought, *I'll no longer be working for Jesus. Jerusalem will offer me something much better,* he was sure.

CHAPTER 4

John, the baptizer, imprisoned.

The palace-fortress at Machaerus sat on a precipice high above the Dead Sea. Originally constructed by Herod the Great as a defensive, military outpost to guard against eastern invaders, Herod Antipas, the son, had extensively renovated the fortress into a lavish palace. A two-story, three-sided building surrounded an interior, open courtyard where Herod presided over parties, banquets, and military drills.

Beneath a large portion of the building, chambers had been created in cavities of the quarried stone used to build two citadel towers and the perimeter walls. Thus, these rooms were enclosed on three sides by solid rock with a stone floor, while ceilings were built with heavy timbers to support the floors above. The deepest and most remote of these damp, sunless chambers had an iron bar front wall and locked gate. After his arrest, John the baptizer was confined in that dark dungeon without a word of explanation.

Once or twice a day, a guard brought food and water to John, though barely enough to keep the baptizer alive.

He slept on a straw mat on the stone floor with only a thin blanket to cover himself. From the little he had been told, he had no idea if he would be granted a trial, or what the charges against him might be. However, John was well aware that he had publicly rebuked Herod Antipas for taking Herodias as his wife. She had been Herod's brother's wife first.

Queen Herodias hated the baptizer, and not just because he had widely condemned her marriage to the king. She regarded John as a filthy, ignorant, deranged hermit who wore animal skins, never trimmed his hair or beard, but sat in self-righteous judgment of all the people of Judea, warning them to repent their sins and submit to his ridiculous immersions in the Jordan. *What a fool,* she thought of him. *I divorced Philip before I married Herod. Who is that absurd troublemaker to tell me I have sinned?*

It was Herodias who convinced Herod Antipas to arrest and imprison John in retribution for his public condemnation of their marriage. She didn't want that wild man telling his foolish followers that she, the queen, was not a legitimate wife.

Now it was Herod's birthday, and a large, lavish party had been planned. Herodias was content knowing the king's feast and celebration would please her. *Too bad that awful creature is alive beneath my footsteps,* she thought. *The king should have imprisoned him in Jerusalem. Nevertheless, I will not let his presence spoil my pleasure of this evening.*

In a dungeon dimly lit during the day and nearly black at night, John was well-prepared for his confinement. Living in desert solitude, he had mastered the art of being alone without the desolate ache of loneliness. He was a man of deep holiness. His thoughts were of God and his own ministry as precursor of the one to come. His prayers were in praise of the glory and goodness of God; his recollections delighted in the beauty of King David's psalms, while his memories dwelt on his happy boyhood with his parents and his beloved cousin, Jesus.

Then, high above, he heard commotion with the arrival of the first guests. He had no idea this evening was King Herod's birthday celebration.

CHAPTER 5

Jesus & Judas in Ephraim.

After learning of John's arrest and imprisonment, Jesus and the twelve withdrew to the town of Ephraim. There, far from the Jordan River valley and its busy road that sloped down from the Sea of Galilee in the north to the town of Bethany beyond the Jordan, Jesus and his friends felt sufficiently removed from the reach of Herod's soldiers.

All were greatly saddened, concerned, and curious about the baptizer's plight. Even Judas Iscariot gave that appearance in his face and utterances. However, in his heart he felt relief in not having to deal with John at the Jordan. He convinced himself that if Jesus learned Judas had lied to him, Jesus would send him away in shame. Judas did not want to suffer that, so he was actually relieved, though not glad, to learn that John had been imprisoned.

Regarding the possible arrest of Jesus and the eleven, Judas thought it unlikely. He didn't understand why Jesus and the others were so frightened. Jesus wasn't a criminal. He hadn't publicly condemned the marriage of Herod and Herodias to earn the wrath of the king. Judas, like the others, indeed like all the crowds that came to hear Jesus teach, recognized him as a remarkably generous and wise man. *So why,* Judas wondered, *was everyone so fearful?*

Nevertheless, Judas conceived a plan to abandon Jesus and the eleven if necessary. He was disappointed Jesus had not yet indicated when he would be going again to Jerusalem. That had been foremost in Judas's mind ever since he left Kerioth several years ago. Now that he could read and write—and how proud he was for it—he was sure he could find employment in Jerusalem. He decided if Jesus would not go soon, then Judas would set out on his own.

The issue of the purse bothered him constantly. Judas felt with complete legitimacy that he did more work to sustain all of them than the other eleven combined. For it, he received no more or less than any of the others, which struck Judas as profoundly unjust. It bothered him, when only a few coins remained in his purse after making the required purchases, that Jesus would pilfer, giving all to whatever beggars they happened to come across. Judas often regretted that he hadn't kept his old water bag. In it, he could have regularly stashed away a few coins for himself. Then, if he did head to Jerusalem on his own, at least he'd have some money. Without funds, he knew, he'd have to rely on his special skill or begging. However, having traveled with Jesus and the others for some time now, he no longer felt like a beggar. Somehow, begging for Jesus' provisions seemed to Judas more honorable. Perhaps it was because he used that money not merely for himself, but for the Teacher and his friends, indifferent as they were.

After they settled in Ephraim, Judas felt content. He'd bide his time. Circumstances, he was sure, would dictate his future path, a path he was certain would lead him to the Holy City on a hill.

CHAPTER 6

The death of John, the baptizer.

Festivities of Herod's birthday celebration in the palace courtyard were raucous and loud. John could not sleep for the din of conversation, boisterous laughter, and a constant drum beat of music. On his back, he stared at the high, timbered ceiling for hours, all the while praying and wondering what his fate might be.

In a room high above John, Herodias was scheming with her seventeen-year-old daughter, Salome.

"I want you to dance for the king and his guests. Will you?"

"I'd be happy to," Salome answered.

"I want you to wear these." Herodias handed her several sheer veils.

"Why, Mother, they'll see my body. . . ."

"I want them to. I want every man who watches you, including the king, to lust after your youth and beauty."

"Why?"

"Because I want you to learn the power you possess over men, even a king. Once you understand that, and

33

use your powers wisely, you, too, might become a queen. If not, then at least the wife of a very rich man. You see, my daughter, men cannot resist a beautiful woman, especially one as luscious as you. Understand that the lust in men's hearts is so powerful that every man here tonight will desire to take you into his bed."

"Am I to go?"

"Absolutely not! Not even the king's bed, though he dare not ask. Never give yourself freely. Always exact a great price because your body and the pleasure it affords are very great indeed."

"I understand, Mother. Oh, I truly do want to become a queen, just like you."

"Good! Now, down the stairs! Go to the king. Tell him you wish to dance for him as a birthday treat."

Deep below, John became aware that the courtyard gathering above had grown quiet, the music more languid, more sensuous. After a long while, there came an eruption of applause and cheers. Then, slowly, the din of conversation returned, but John heard no more laughter and no more music. Finally, he fell asleep.

Several men with torches descended the steps to John's cell. Commotion at the unlocking of the iron bar gate startled John awake. One man ripped the blanket off John. Two others pulled him up and tied his hands behind his back.

"What's happening?" John asked, trembling with fear.

No one answered. They dragged him up the stairs, down a hallway, and into a stone chamber similar to his own. John, sensing great danger, shivered uncontrollably.

Ananias, a man powerfully built and exuding authority, said, "Stand in front of that stone block."

John glanced around the chamber, lit by wall torches. Two other men drew near him.

"Tie him up," the man ordered.

They bound his arms to his torso with heavy rope, then forced him to kneel. They tied his ankles together, and his upper legs.

When John glanced again at Ananias, he spotted a long sword leaning against the wall behind Ananias. Horrified, he realized what was to come. An overpowering fear possessed John's entire being. Within the heavy ropes he shivered violently.

"No, no . . . I beg of you. . . ."

"King's orders," Ananias said. "I have no choice. . . ."

"No, please, no. . . ."

"Calm yourself now."

John groaned a deep, pathetic sound.

Ananias knelt by John. "I'm going to position your head over the edge of the stone. Look straight down at the pan on the floor. Keep it right there!"

"No, I beg of you . . . no, no. . . ."

"If not your head, it will be mine," Ananias said. "What would you do in my situation?"

"No. . . ."

"Keep your head down and still. Try to calm yourself."

John, moaning and nearly insane with fear, said nothing.

"You holy men are always telling people to trust in God. Well, now it's time for *you* to trust in God."

"I do," John said.

Ananias placed his large, hard hands on John's upper back. "Calm yourself."

"I'm cold."

Turning to one of the other men, Ananias ordered him to fetch a blanket. He returned with a heavy, horse blanket that Ananias placed over John's shivering body, still clothed only in the animal skin he wore since before he was arrested.

"Try to calm yourself," he repeated.

"I am," John said.

John closed his eyes, begging God for strength to endure his overwhelming terror. In his mind the Psalmist's words raced over and over: *To you I lift up my soul, O Lord. In you I trust.*

Again Ananias knelt by John's head. "You baptized my sister. She wanted me to go to you and repent my sins and be baptized, but I never did."

"Seek Jesus of Nazareth . . . your sister, too . . . follow him now."

"Perhaps I wouldn't be here had I come to you."

"Then someone else would kill me," John said.

"Forgive me, baptizer, for what I must do."

"There is nothing for me to forgive. You wield the sword, but it is Herod who murders me. Tell your sister: it isn't your sin, only Herod's."

A messenger sent down from the courtyard rushed into the chamber. "Hurry," he said. "The king grows restless."

"Close your eyes now, baptizer, and listen to me," Ananias said. "My sword is heavy; its blade exceedingly sharp. My downward stroke is swift as lightning. You will feel nothing, no pain, no suffering. It's over in an instant. And in the next instant, baptizer, you will be with God." He stood. Another handed him the sword.

John whispered, "With God, yes . . . with God-"

John's head dropped into the pan and rolled sideways away from twin blood streams that shot from his cleanly cut carotid arteries.

The king's steward lifted John's severed head by its hair, placing it on a silver platter. He rushed up the long flight of stone stairs to the waiting king and courtyard.

When Salome saw the head of the baptizer, she screamed in horror, while her mother, Queen Herodias, laughed gleefully in triumph.

CHAPTER 7

To Jerusalem.

More than one hundred men—ministers from Jerusalem, high officials from nearby towns, military commanders, important tribesmen, and wealthy merchants—attended King Herod's birthday celebration. In addition, at least half that number, comprised of palace guards, stewards, and servant girls, were also present in the courtyard when the plated, bloody head of John, the baptizer, was presented to Salome.

Thus, news of John's beheading spread throughout the whole of Judaea, Samaria, and Galilee with the speed of a thousand arrows loosed by a cohort of archers from the high parapets of Machaerus. Traveler to traveler, details of the gruesome execution were passed.

In early afternoon of the second day after the murder of his cousin, Jesus learned of it while still in Ephraim. His twelve friends were stunned and horrified by the news.

Jesus went off by himself and wept.

John, one of the twelve, said, "God gave Moses the command, *Thou shalt not kill.* To kill another is a great evil, we all know that, but to behead another is the mutilation of a Temple of the Holy Spirit. Woe to such a man."

"So King Herod is evil," Judas said.

"Of course he is," John replied.

"Then why is he king?" Peter asked. "Why must we Jews endure an evil king?"

John said, "That is why the people of Israel long for the coming of the Messiah."

"Do you think Jesus will stay here?" Andrew, Peter's brother, asked.

"No," Philip said, "I think he'll want to go to Capernaum, much safer up there."

"I hope so," Peter said. "I'd like to visit my wife and sleep in my own bed for a change."

The others laughed. Peter's wife lived in Bethsaida, not far from Capernaum at the north end of the Sea of Galilee.

"Jesus enjoys the seashore," Andrew said. "We'll go there. I'm sure of it."

"I'll wager you, Brother, we stay here," Peter said. "Believe me, Jesus does not have the same interest in my wife's bed that I have."

They all laughed again until they heard Jesus' booming voice call, "Judas!"

Jesus approached the twelve. "How much in the purse, Judas?"

"A few denarii," he answered.

"Go, spend it all for food and fill your water bag."

Judas went off.

"All of you go fill your water bags. As soon as Judas returns we're leaving."

Judas stopped when he heard it. He called back to Jesus, "Where are we going?"

"Jerusalem," Jesus said. "At last, Jerusalem!"

CHAPTER 8

Two women to Jerusalem.

The holy city on a hill that Judas Iscariot yearned to see, divided unequally into four parts. In the northeast quadrant, smallest, but most impressive, was Herod's Temple whose east foundation wall rose fortress-like above the deep Kidron Valley. South of the Temple lay the old City of David, established by the great king a thousand years earlier. West of and adjacent to David's city was the Lower City in the Tyropoeon Valley. Further west, beyond and above a long, separating ridge, the Upper City comprised about half the area within the outer defense walls. Concentrated there, the wealth of Jerusalem was most apparent with its fine palaces, residences, abundant markets, and Roman theater. In the northwest corner at its highest point, the palace-fortress of Herod the Great dominated with its three tall towers: the Tower of Phasael, named for his brother; Hippicus, named for a friend; and Mariamme, named for his wife whom he murdered.

Two women also yearned to see Jerusalem, but, unlike Judas, not for its physical splendor and riches. Travelers from the south brought news to Mary in Nazareth that her son planned to spend the Passover festival week in Jerusalem. She hadn't seen Jesus in over a year, so she decided, even though she was growing older, to make again the long journey to see her beloved son. Mary prepared her few things, then joined a small caravan from Galilee heading toward Jerusalem. They wouldn't arrive early in the week, but she would certainly be there before Passover, which she hoped to share with Jesus and his friends.

Another woman named Mary, originally from the fishing village of Magdala on the northwest shore of the Sea of Galilee, also learned that Jesus would be in Jerusalem for festival week. Born into poverty, abandoned at a young age, desperately alone, hungry, and always poor, she had become a woman of ill repute. When Jesus befriended her, she abandoned her old ways and became a follower of his teachings.

When she first encountered the Nazarene, when he spoke to her, when he peered into her eyes, she felt a sense of being loved that she had never once experienced from the aggregate of men to whom she had sold her body. After hearing him tell of a kingdom of meekness and mercy, of justice and peace, words spoken with authority and strength, she knew in her heart that if she could ever get to know this man she would love him.

The hard shell that enclosed her heart since her abysmal girlhood had been broken forever. No longer was she a common prostitute, desperate in a wretched hovel. She changed her life, abandoned her past ways, and though she had been a woman scorned and shunned, she became a welcomed follower of Jesus, a disciple of the wandering Galilean teacher. In her heart she yearned to experience again and again the love that flowed so abundantly from his entire personality. She determined to meet him, to get to know him, to become his friend. In the secret places of her heart, when she allowed the power of her femininity to come to the fore of her thinking, she realized she longed to be more than his friend. With the men who bought her body she had withheld her heart. She never allowed herself to fully express her sexuality because it represented the deepest and most profound essence of her desire to love and be loved, something she never once experienced with the rough, vulgar men who had no interest in her soul.

After hearing Jesus teach, she left Magdala and went to dwell in the town of Capernaum where Jesus often taught at synagogue. From this small fishing village he called his first followers: Andrew and Peter, James and John. A tax collector named Matthew worked at the customs house on the main road from Damascus to the Mediterranean Sea. He, too, became a follower of Jesus, and within a small garrison of Roman soldiers stationed there, most had also become followers of Jesus.

Magdalene, as she now was called, befriended women in the town, wives of fishermen and others who were drawn to the teachings of the Nazarene. She found work in the house of a garment seamstress who admired Magdalene's natural skill with needle, thread, and Egyptian scissors.

Now in haste she left her little room in the home of the seamstress and headed for Jerusalem where she longed to encounter Jesus again.

Jesus, however, instead of going straight to Jerusalem, decided to visit his friends, Lazarus and his sisters, Martha and Mary, in Bethany, a short distance from the Holy City. Jesus and his companions would spend the night there. Early on the morning of the Sabbath they would cross the Kidron Valley and then climb the winding slope to Jerusalem.

Judas was not pleased. To him it seemed like just another delay after countless delays. Nevertheless, being so close to his ultimate destination, he agreed to remain with Jesus and the others. The long wait to finally see Jerusalem built an almost fearful anticipation in his mind. He hoped the city held some kind of opportunity for him. *But what?* he wondered. Wandering around Galilee, Samaria, and Judea, as well as up and down the Jordan River valley, had become tiresome and tedious.

In Judas's mind and in fact, he had provided Jesus and his friends with a great deal of food, clothing, and shelter. Yet, he was as poor as the day he met them. *All that work and for what?* he pondered. After festival week, he presumed, when Jesus and his friends were intending to leave the Holy City, Judas would stay behind. That thought gave him odd pleasure, though he had no real sense of what work he could do. He certainly wouldn't allow himself to become a common beggar, nor would he steal, except perhaps to eat, when necessary. He wanted something that utilized his ability to read and write, something to reward his imagined cleverness and ambition, though he had no idea what that might possibly be.

"Welcome Teacher," Lazarus said, rushing to meet Jesus at his courtyard gate. "I'm delighted to see you, as are my sisters."

"Oh, yes, yes," Martha and Mary said, smiling joyfully.

"And welcome to your friends," Lazarus said.

"You all must have supper with us," Martha declared. "We'll make room."

"We will," Jesus said. "But in the morning we leave for Jerusalem."

"Our guest room, with fresh linens, is well prepared for you tonight, Master," Martha said. "Your friends, though, will have to sleep in the courtyard."

Jesus smiled. "They're used to sleeping beneath the stars."

"I'll build them a big fire," Lazarus said.

"Come, Mary! We must cook for these hungry fellows."

Jesus, Lazarus, and the others mingled in the courtyard, or reclined on benches under a spreading fig tree until the sisters announced supper was ready.

When the meal was finished, Mary asked Jesus, "Will you come back tomorrow evening?"

"Yes, though probably not until late. We'll sup in Jerusalem then return here."

Mary said, "Will you join us for the Passover meal? It would be wonderful to celebrate with you."

"No, Mary. I promised my friends we'd celebrate in the Holy City. It's important for me, for all of us, to be there."

"I'm disappointed in you," Martha said. "Jerusalem is so crowded and dirty."

Mary added, "Here it's quiet and peaceful and the weather is fair. We'll talk and tell stories, and you can teach us more about the Kingdom of God."

"And we could get to know your friends better, too," Martha said.

"No, Martha. We will be in Jerusalem."

Lazarus told his sisters, "Stop pleading! Do not try to dissuade the Master."

That early Sabbath morning, Jesus with the twelve left Bethany, heading for Jerusalem along the road that passed the Mount of Olives. When they reached the path leading to the summit, Jesus turned and began climbing. The others followed.

Judas muttered, "Now where is he taking us?"

"You'll see," Matthew said.

From a narrow clearing among groves of olive trees that dressed the mountain, the whole of Jerusalem in brilliant morning sunlight spread out in front of and below them. The Temple precinct's massive, east retaining wall, its sandstone resplendent in a rosy, golden glow, towered above the Kidron Valley.

"There Judas," Jesus said, pointing, "is the city you're so anxious to claim. What do you think of it? Is it what you imagined?"

But Judas's imagination was too myopic, too uncultivated to ever have been able to anticipate the marvelous vision of the ancient, modern city that lay before his incredulous gaze.

"It's large," he said. "I had no idea it was so large."

"Do you see the tall, stone wall nearest us that rises above the Kidron valley; and do you see the open courtyard beyond?"

"Yes," Judas answered.

"The high building within is the Temple."

"What are those three tall towers in the distance?" Judas asked.

"That's the palace of King Herod."

". . . Antipas?" Judas asked.

"No, his father, Herod the Great."

"Why was he called *Great?*"

"Because he built most of the grandeur that you see."

Peter said, "He was a murderer, a killer of innocents; he killed his own wife."

"Enough," Jesus said.

"This grandeur doesn't mean dung in God's eyes."

"I said *enough*, Peter. No more of Herod!"

Jesus turned and headed back down the mountain. Along with young Judas and the others, the time had come to once again cross over to the Holy City.

CHAPTER 9

A Jerusalem dinner party.

Jesus entered Jerusalem through the eastern gate of the Temple mount where he was greeted by noisy, friendly crowds: inhabitants, for the most part, of the old City of David and the Lower City. Poor women and their children came, as did the elderly sick and lame, weary laborers and humble beggars, all outcasts from the wealthy precincts of Jerusalem's Upper City. They had heard remarkable stories about Jesus, his teachings, and his wondrous acts of healing. Now they wanted to see him. When they finally did, they shouted *Hosanna* and waved palm branches in the fresh, morning air, hoping he'd glance their way.

In this large crowd, a wealthy merchant and member of the Sanhedrin, Joseph of Arimathea, waited to greet Jesus personally. He had met Jesus and learned his radical teachings several years earlier, becoming an ardent, but secret follower. Nevertheless, now openly, he was anxious to invite Jesus to his house for the evening meal.

"I've room for six. Two other members of the Sanhedrin

are coming, and I've also invited a merchant acquaintance. They're all anxious to meet you."

"That makes five," Jesus said.

"You may bring a guest. Bring one of your friends."

After spending most of the day in the Temple precincts teaching, answering questions, and speaking with all who approached him, Jesus, with a friend he asked to come along, strode through the streets of the Upper City toward the house of the Arimathean.

"I came to Jerusalem, Judas, because she, too, more than the whole of Judea, needs to hear the good news. Wherever you go, whatever you see, whomever you meet, remember that. There are many righteous here, but many who dwell in darkness."

"The righteous welcomed you this morning, hundreds of them."

"Ah, the poor and lowly, but where were the rich and powerful?"

"Some were there. That man you talked to. . . ."

"Yes, but thousands of rich men dwell here, Judas."

"I like Jerusalem." "It's exciting, busy, lots of people."

"It has always been my destination and my destiny," Jesus said. "Perhaps, your destiny, too."

"What do you mean?"

"I mean if you choose to live and work in Jerusalem."

The comment surprised and pleased Judas. That

suggestion, an idea he held for a long time, intrigued and excited him. "Yes, maybe I will."

"Well, whatever you eventually decide, Judas, this evening we dine at a rich man's table."

"I'm surprised you asked me. I thought you'd ask Peter or John or one of the others. I know you love them more."

"No, I love you all equally."

Judas didn't believe it. For many months he had observed how much more Jesus enjoyed conversing with his other friends. Rarely did Jesus engage Judas in anything other than matters of the purse. He felt they all looked at him as not being particularly smart. He hated that.

"You have kept us fed and clothed, Judas. To show my appreciation, I invited you to join me this evening. Our host has room for only two, not thirteen."

"The others are better talkers than me."

"That's true, but you're younger; you haven't experienced life, as they have. You still have much to learn."

"Someday I'd like a wife. . . ."

"Our wanderings will end soon enough. Then you'll have time to find a young woman to marry and have children. That will be good for you."

"I want a wife in Jerusalem."

"Perhaps, but remember: while a holy city because of its history and sacred Temple, Jerusalem has many who are not God-fearing, who do not live by the commands of

God and Moses. This is a city, Judas, where one must be careful not to be seduced by worldly attractions, whether food or wine, a love of money and fame, or lust for its beautiful women."

"I had no time for courting in the country towns we went to."

"I understand, but learn how Jerusalem works before you decide anything. See how you like it after this coming week."

"I'll still like it; I know I will. I can read and write, so I should be of use to someone."

"Judas, I understand, but remember: be on guard for those who might seem your friend, but would just as soon lead you astray."

That's not going to happen, Judas thought. *I'm sick of begging for Jesus and his lazy friends. Talk about leading astray. From now on the money I earn, I keep for myself. He and his friends can beg for the rest of their lives without me. See how they like that.*

Joseph's house in Jerusalem was not large, but well-built and comfortable. As a member of the Sanhedrin, he often had to leave his native place and come to the Holy City where he desired a familiar dwelling with its own kitchen. A cook and two servant girls were available on short notice.

On many occasions over the years, Joseph had

entertained guests for a meal and serious conversation. This Sunday evening he would do the same for a group that included a man Joseph greatly admired, a teacher of great wisdom and power.

"Let me present my good friend, Nicodemus. And this is Saul who comes from the town of Tarsus. Both are members of the Sanhedrin. This is Simon of Jerusalem, a merchant acquaintance of mine. Gentlemen, I'm honored to introduce Jesus of Nazareth and his young friend, Judas Iscariot."

The men shook hands, while wishing one another *Peace.*

They conversed in generalities until Joseph and Nicodemus engaged Jesus to the exclusion of the others. Simon suggested to Saul and Judas that they withdraw to the inner courtyard. "The evening air is pleasant," he said.

"So, Judas, tell us, what exactly do you do for Jesus?" Saul asked.

"I keep the purse."

"How do you earn money? How many in your group to support?" Simon asked.

"Thirteen," Judas said. "I beg among the crowds that come to hear Jesus."

"Do any of the others beg with you?"

"No, I'm the only one."

"Does Jesus pay you?" Simon asked.

"No."

"That doesn't seem very fair," Saul said.

"It's not," Judas said. "It isn't easy to constantly beg yet have no say in how money is spent. Jesus doles it out; he tells me when to buy food. If someone needs something he approves or denies it. He even gives to beggars. I do all the begging, but have no control at all."

Simon inquired, "Judas, you mentioned that Jesus was a carpenter. I thought he was a vintner, a wine maker."

"I never heard that," Judas said. "Before he was a teacher, he was a carpenter. His father was a carpenter."

"How does one go from being a carpenter to being a teacher?" Saul asked. "Carpentry is a trade of the hands; teaching a trade of the mind."

"I don't know, but he taught me how to read and write. Why would you think he was a wine maker?"

Simon said, "I have a friend whose son is a merchant. I had supper at their home several years ago, and this son told an interesting story. He travels throughout Samaria and Galilee selling his wares—kitchen items, housewares, cloth, those kinds of things. He came to the little town of Cana in Galilee. He had sold his wares there before, so many townspeople knew him. That particular day, he arrived rather late, toward evening. A wedding feast had occurred, but when he arrived most of the guests, as well as the bride and groom, had left. Young men, rowdy from too much wine, invited him to join the festivities. They offered him a cup of blood-red wine, which he gladly enjoyed having come from a house where his father often served fine wine. Well, he told us it was the finest wine he ever tasted. So he asked one of the stewards where the wine came from. He said Jesus of Nazareth had furnished it, in fact, furnished six large water jugs of it, enough to keep the town drunk for a week."

All three men laughed.

"I never heard such a story," Judas said. "None of his friends ever mentioned that. Jesus doesn't say much about his past life; he rarely talks about himself."

Saul said, "You told us Jesus taught you to read and write."

"Yes."

"You'll need that in Jerusalem."

"What are your plans, Judas?" Simon asked. "After Passover week will you still follow your wandering Nazarene preacher?"

Judas corrected the man. "Not a preacher, a teacher, a real teacher, a *Rabbi*.

"Oh, excuse me," Simon said, grinning at Saul.

"No, I want to work in Jerusalem. I'm tired of roaming all over the countryside. I'd like to settle down here, maybe even get married someday."

Simon asked, "Does Jesus know your plans?"

"Yes, work and marriage."

"Judas," Simon said, "I might have some work for you. If you're interested, come see me tomorrow morning. I have a stall in the Temple Court of the Gentiles. Ask anyone to point you to it. I'm well known."

Surprised and pleased at an offer so easily and quickly given, Judas said, "I will."

Their Arimathean host appeared in the doorway. "Gentlemen, our supper is served."

CHAPTER 10

The return to Bethany.

Two servant girls placed large trays of steaming fish and sauce so all six could easily reach them; also brought were baskets of freshly baked bread with small plates of olive oil for dipping. Other delicacies included stewed lentils, herbed olives, and bowls of dried figs and dates. For the men's thirst, four large jugs of red wine were set in a row. The beautifully presented food made a tremendous impression on Judas. He had never seen anything like it.

The comely serving girls seized his attention even more. He tried to catch their glances, but their eyes were constantly drawn to the handsome, honored, Galilean guest rather than to a swarthy faced man from Kerioth.

Jesus offered a prayer of thanksgiving before the leisurely dining began. None, however, had Judas's robust appetite. Because his lack of experience and knowledge prevented him from fully participating in conversation, he ate with a casual indifference to what was being discussed. He found every morsel delicious and, after a mouthful or

two, the wine even more so. He ate with such obvious pleasure that the other men noticed it with amusement, but
made no comment before resuming their conversations.

Plateful after plateful Judas devoured, literally stuffing
himself, while gulping cupful after cupful of wine.

Nearing the end of the meal, the Arimathean com-
mented to Jesus, "Your young friend has quite an appetite..."

"Yes," Jesus said. "I've starved him for a long time."

"... and a fondness for my wine."

"Let him enjoy the pleasures of wine this evening. In
the morning he'll learn its pain."

Overhearing Jesus, Simon asked, "I heard from a friend
that years ago you were a wine maker. Is that true?"

Jesus laughed. "For a while I had that reputation, but
I was the son of a carpenter and learned that trade and
worked at it until I began my public ministry."

Surprising everyone, Judas slurred, "That's what I told
them."

"Stand up," Jesus commanded.

With great difficulty, Judas rose to his feet. He swayed
noticeably. Other men stood, while backing away from
Judas.

In the entry court Jesus thanked Joseph and apologized
for Judas's overindulgence.

"Why don't you spend the night here?" the Arimathean
asked.

"I promised my friends in Bethany we'd return."

"It's late and there's always the likelihood of bandits."

"We'll be safe," Jesus said.

Through the Upper City's darkened streets, across the masonry arch causeway leading to Temple precincts, and finally out the east gate past the night guards, Jesus struggled to hold up a staggering, stumbling Judas. Down the winding path to the floor of the Kidron Valley, Jesus caught Judas from falling three times. When they reached the creek bed, Jesus knew it was impossible to continue on like this. Using his carpenter's strength, he lifted and slung Judas over his right shoulder, adjusted their combined weight to gain balance, then began walking at a faster pace on the road to Bethany.

Approaching the sleepy town, several lit lamps, two at the house of Lazarus, guided Jesus.

Martha and Mary were waiting, but seeing Jesus carrying Judas shocked them both.

"What's wrong with him?" Martha asked.

"Too much wine," Jesus answered. "Let me put him down. He'll sleep the night, but I think he could use a blanket."

Mary went to fetch one.

"He's drunk," Martha said. "What a disgrace. Has he no idea who you are?"

"A youthful indiscretion, that's all."

Mary handed the blanket to Jesus who covered Judas tenderly, as though Judas was his son.

"You're too good to him," Martha said. "I never liked him from the first time you brought him here. He's not good enough to be one of your friends."

"Martha, who are you to judge?"

Realizing how wrong it was to speak that way to Jesus, she said, "I'm sorry, Master. Forgive me. I'm very tired. Good night."

"Sleep well," Jesus said, as Martha withdrew.

In the dimly lit courtyard, Jesus turned toward Mary who gazed at him with an intense look of love and longing. "May I show you to your room?"

"No," Jesus said. "I know the way."

CHAPTER II

Judas at the house of Lazarus.

Judas woke several hours after Jesus, with the others, left for Jerusalem. Under an intense high sun, dehydrated, hungry, confused, and feeling extremely sick with headache, Judas wondered how he came to sleep beside a dead fire at the base of a wall enclosing Lazarus's courtyard.

He squinted to see Martha and Mary hanging laundry. When Martha noticed him stirring she said, ". . . about time you wake. Get up! I want you out of here."

Judas struggled to his feet.

"I filled your water bag," Mary said, pointing.

Judas picked it up and drank, nearly emptying it. "Where's Jesus?"

"They left early," Mary said. "Jesus told us to let you sleep."

"I'm hungry."

"That's your problem," Martha said.

Mary went into the house and returned with a chunk of bread, handing it to Judas. "Give me your water bag. I'll fill it."

"He's got to leave," Martha said.

Judas knew she didn't like him. "I'll go," he said, "but can I finish my bread?"

"Yes," Mary said. "Sit in the shade. No need to rush."

"Mary," Martha snapped, "I want him out of here. Don't you understand that?"

Lazarus appeared in the doorway. "Judas, finish eating and then leave. I don't like seeing my sister upset, and you've no reason to stay here. I'm sure Jesus wants you in Jerusalem as soon as possible."

"You're not our friend," Martha said in a nasty tone.

"Martha," Mary said, "not so harsh."

"Well, he's not. Why Jesus has him I'll never understand."

"I'll go now," Judas said after eating. "I know when I'm not wanted."

He gathered his cloak, placing his water bag in a deep pocket, and passed by the three of them without saying another word.

"Good riddance," Martha said, loud enough for Judas to hear.

"Really, Martha," Lazarus said, "I understand you don't like the man, but there's no reason to be unkind. He's a human being; you don't know what his life has been. Surely you could have hid your dislike for the little time he was here."

"You're right, I suppose," Martha said, "but there's something about him that makes me very uncomfortable. He's not like Jesus' other friends. If nothing else he seems . . . ," she paused searching for the right word, "sinister."

CHAPTER 12

Judas visits Simon, a merchant.

Judas disliked Martha as much as she disliked him. She made him feel small and worthless, just as the townsfolk of Kerioth did a decade earlier. He resolved not to return to Bethany even if Jesus commanded it, though he doubted Jesus would force him. And if he did, it would be an opportunity for Judas to finally break from Jesus and his band. Now, half way to Jerusalem, Judas remembered that Simon the Merchant invited him to his stall.

"Where the hell have you been?" Simon barked. "Didn't I tell you to come in the morning?"

"Bethany. I overslept."

"You overslept because you got drunk last night. You ate like a pig and drank that man's fine wine like water. You did not make a good impression on anyone, least of all me. You should be ashamed of yourself, especially for getting drunk in the presence of those distinguished men."

Judas, deeply humiliated, realized that Simon condemned him for the same boorish behavior that Judas, countless times as a boy, detested in his own drunken father. He could not defend or dispute his own behavior—good or bad—because he had difficulty recalling it. He enjoyed the food and wine greatly because it was the finest meal he had ever eaten. But now, regardless of how he tried, he could not remember leaving the Arimathean's house, nor could he recollect how he got to Lazarus's courtyard.

Simon saw the shame in Judas's expression. "Your Jesus called it 'youthful indiscretion.' He's too forgiving. I call it disgusting."

Judas did not respond; he stood staring at the floor, wondering if he had destroyed his chance to work for the merchant.

"A word of warning, Judas. If you end up working for me, and right now that's not certain, I don't ever want you getting drunk again, understand?"

"Yes."

"Good. Now I want to talk about your Jesus. Did you notice how few people are in the Temple precincts today?"

Simon's change of topic eased Judas's discomfort. "I've never really been here before."

"Oh, that's right; you said yesterday was your first day. Well, usually, especially during festival week, the precincts are crowded with people, many of them pilgrims. They come to exchange their money for Jerusalem money. The poor come to buy sacrificial doves for the Temple offering. The rich come to buy lambs. These have been Temple traditions for hundreds of years."

"What's that got to do with Jesus?" Judas asked.

"Jesus was here earlier. You should have been with me to witness the show he put on. I could hardly believe it was the same man we had supper with last evening."

"I don't understand. What are you talking about?"

"This morning, while you slept off your drunken stupor, Jesus came in here like a wild man. He had a whip, Judas, and with it he drove out the money-changers and dove sellers. He overturned tables filled with coins; money scattered everywhere. Everyone scrambled to pick it up. Merchants panicked trying to recover what was rightfully theirs. Yet he whipped any merchant who refused to leave. And all the while he's screaming that the Temple is his father's house, and these money-changers had turned it into a den of thieves. It was a scene of total, utter chaos."

"That doesn't sound like Jesus," Judas said.

"Obviously, you don't know the man. I never saw anything like it. I've never seen anyone act in such a blatantly criminal way, and yet no one resisted, let alone tried to stop him. The Temple guards did nothing, stood there as though they were too afraid to do what they're supposed to do."

"What's that?"

"Judas, don't ask stupid questions. What the hell do you think guards are supposed to do? They should have arrested him, but they did nothing—worthless cowards."

"What did you do?" Judas asked.

Simon did not expect lowly Judas, of all people, to question him. He resented it, for he regarded himself as a truly superior man. Nevertheless, Simon had, in fact, done nothing but watch, for he, too, felt fear at the fury of Jesus' anger. "Well, I was going to fetch some Roman soldiers, but another merchant went ahead of me."

"What did the Romans do?"

"They never came. They told the merchant the Temple was the domain of Jews. It's up to Temple guards to control things."

"Where is Jesus now?" Judas asked.

"Good question. He creates a general havoc, then disappears. The merchants came back, though, collected their things and left. But tomorrow, despite all the trouble and misery Jesus caused, the buying and selling will start again. So, Judas, what good did your Jesus accomplish by causing all this destruction?"

Judas did not respond. Simon returned to his comfortable chair and motioned for Judas to sit next to him.

"Now, Judas, let's talk about you, but in a more pleasant manner. Last evening, you told me you handle the purse for Jesus. Do you like begging for money?"

"No," Judas answered. "I hate it."

"Do you like money? Are you comfortable handling it?"

"Yes, I am."

"Anyone with a good head for money does well in Jerusalem. You and your roaming rabbi scratch and beg for a few coins from those just as poor as yourselves. But here, Judas, you'd be surprised how much money you could earn with a relatively small amount of work."

"I don't understand. . . ."

"I'm a merchant, Judas, but I don't buy and sell goods. I deal in something intangible, but also far more valuable."

"What's that?" Judas asked.

"In a city this large and this complex with competing political and merchant rivalries, knowledge and information become very valuable. If a man keeps his eyes and ears open, learns whatever he can about important people and events, then there's always someone willing to pay for that information."

"I see," Judas said, with little conviction.

"What do you think is the most precious thing in Jerusalem?"

"Money, gold, silver, jewels, things like that."

"Yes, that's what most people who don't understand Jerusalem would say. But it's not true. The most precious thing in Jerusalem and the whole of Judea is information, Judas. Information!

"I'll give you an example: suppose the Assyrians are preparing their army to lay siege against Jerusalem. Do you think knowing that in advance would be of value to the Romans, to Herod, to all the people of Jerusalem?"

"Yes, of course," Judas answered.

"So, you see how information really is the most precious thing in Jerusalem."

"I suppose so," Judas replied.

"It's not something you suppose about." Simon, shaking his head in exasperation, realized Judas possessed little worldly experience and less understanding, so he asked, "What are you doing the rest of today?"

"I want to get to know Jerusalem better."

"Good. Walk her streets, check out the markets, visit the palace of Herod the Great. Enjoy yourself."

"I will," Judas said.

"Tomorrow, come here in the morning. Then we'll talk about you possibly working for me."

"Alright."

"Keep in mind what I told you. Don't get drunk if you want to work for me."

"I'll remember."

"Oh, and Judas, if you fail to come in the morning, don't bother coming at all."

CHAPTER 13

Martha's opinions.

Jesus, with most of his disciples, returned to Bethany in late afternoon. As always, Lazarus and his sisters were delighted to see him.

"We'll prepare supper for you," Martha said, while counting heads. "There's only nine."

"Good," Jesus said. "We're hungry, haven't eaten all day. Peter, Andrew, and James stayed in the city." Turning to Lazarus, he asked, "Is Judas here?"

Martha heard it. "I sent him away. I told him not to come back."

"Why?" Jesus asked.

"He upsets Martha," Lazarus said, "and there's no good reason for him to stay here. I told him you'd want him in Jerusalem."

"Forgive me, Master," Martha began, "but I don't like your Judas. I see no reason why I should have to cook for him."

"Except, perhaps, that he's my friend," Jesus said.

Martha bowed her head. She regretted disappointing

Jesus for failing to be hospitable, but she was adamant in her conviction that she didn't want him in her home. She felt she had that right.

Mary approached Jesus. "I gave him some bread and filled his water bag when he left."

"Good." Jesus smiled at her, then said, "Actually, I suspect Judas prefers to stay in Jerusalem. He wants to get to know the city. He hopes to find work there and, eventually, get married."

Hearing it, Martha scoffed. *What woman in her right mind would marry that crude, terrible man?* she wondered.

CHAPTER 14

A plan and a price.

Samuel, a prominent member of the Sanhedrin, welcomed Simon in one of the small alcoves off the main hall of that governing, religious group. "I detected urgency in your note, my friend. Is something troubling you?" he asked.

"One thing I don't understand," Simon began, "is why Jesus wasn't arrested after causing such mayhem in the Court of the Gentiles?"

"Yes, that was a pathetic scene. We had a chance to arrest him, but there was a terrible failure of leadership on the part of the captain of the Temple Guards."

"Clearly, it was a criminal act," Simon said.

"Of course it was. That crazy Nazarean should have been apprehended then, but the captain failed to order an arrest."

"Why? It was a riot; merchants were stolen from. It makes no sense not to arrest."

"Unless," Samuel said, "the captain was a follower of Jesus, which we discovered upon questioning, he was."

"Oh, I see. So he's even infected the Temple Guards."

"To a limted extent, although that worthless captain has been discharged and disgraced. He no longer serves in any capacity with the Temple Guard, banned for life, actually."

"And rightly so," Simon said.

"Is that all you came for?"

"No," Simon answered. "Let me ask you this: If I could hand Jesus over to the Sanhedrin what would they pay me?"

Samuel chuckled. "What makes you think you could hand over that elusive rascal?"

"I've become acquainted with a follower of Jesus, a young man named Judas from Kerioth in the south. He's young, not terribly smart, and, I suspect, quite malleable in the right hands."

"Your hands, I presume."

"Of course."

"Well, let's talk about what you mean when you say 'hand him over.' You know Jesus has many followers here in Jerusalem for Passover. We can't afford a riot."

"I think there are three essential elements to his arrest, an arrest that must be as non-violent as possible. First, we must be able to attain a positive identification. Young Judas can provide that. Second, it is preferable if the arrest takes place at night when the streets are empty. I'm hoping that he can provide that as well. Third, it would be easier, by that I mean less prone to riot, if it could occur outside the city walls."

"You've thought things out well, Simon. I agree with you."

"So let me ask you again: if I can facilitate the arrest of Jesus, without causing an undue disturbance, what would you be willing to pay?"

"Simon, you're a member of the Sanhedrin. You know how stingy we all are. What would you want?"

"One hundred and fifty pieces of Roman Silver."

"Never," Samuel said. "The full Sanhedrin would never approve that and certainly not to one of our own."

"I know how anxious a large faction of the Sanhedrin is to question Jesus. You're part of that. I think one hundred and fifty silvers is eminently fair."

"Never," Samuel said again. "Yes, we want to question him, but the Sanhedrin simply won't agree to that much."

"What would they agree to?"

"Maybe a hundred, but I'll have to do a lot of arm twisting."

"I was going to pay Judas fifty."

"Is he poor?"

"Yes, very."

"Then pay him thirty pieces. He'll think himself a rich man."

CHAPTER 15

An enjoyable afternoon.

After leaving Simon, Judas descended the staircase to
the Lower City and the sprawling marketplace below
the arched causeway. Observing the crowded alleys and
shops gave him great pleasure. He strolled leisurely, moving with or through throngs of shoppers, while noticing
with keen eyes how foodstuffs were presented. *This is going
to be easy,* he realized.

At a baker's stall, baskets of bread were within easy
reach, although at this late hour, many had been emp-
tied. The baker or his wife removed those or combined
a few remaining loaves with another nearly empty basket,
shoving it forward toward the milling crowd. Judas spotted a small loaf and moved toward it slowly, always eye-
ing what the baker and his wife were doing. Opportunity
came when several women lined up to purchase bread,
occupying the baker and his wife's attention. Judas's quick
left hand snatched the small loaf and dropped it into a
pocket of his cloak. Several stalls away, Judas came upon
a table laden with baskets of dates and figs. A swift swipe

of his right hand dropped a handful into his cloak's other pocket.

Judas, ever suspecting and watchful, glanced all around. No one was looking at him except, perhaps, for a young woman whose gaze met Judas's eyes for an instant, or so he thought. *Was she staring at me?* he wondered. Pushing against a wall of shoppers, he moved toward her, but she had disappeared into the teeming crowd.

Departing the marketplace, Judas went back to the Herodian Staircase that ascended to the two Huldah Gates at the south wall of the Temple precinct. He sat on a high step overlooking the City of David, the oldest and poorest neighborhood in Jerusalem. He ate bread and dates and drank from his fine water bag, enjoying the afternoon sunlight. *I'll eat well in Jerusalem, but not spend a single denarius.* Yet he didn't want to rely on thievery, skillful as he believed he was. He considered himself fortunate to have made the acquaintance of Simon whom he wanted to work for, even though Simon spoke critically of Judas. *But only because I got drunk,* he concluded. *And how does he buy and sell information? How does that work?* Judas wondered.

Judas promised Simon he would not get drunk again, even though Judas truly enjoyed the Arimathean's fine wine. He did not enjoy, however, feeling miserable the next morning. He thought again of his drunken father and all the hated memories of his youth in Kerioth. *My father got drunk almost every night,* Judas recalled, or so it seemed. *I'll never do that,* he resolved. *My father was stupid. I am not.*

After Judas finished eating, he crossed the causeway into the Upper City. He enjoyed all that he observed: many well-dressed people, fine houses and buildings, the Roman Theater, and Herod's Palace with its three tall towers. He tried to recall the location of the Arimathean's house, but could not find it within the maze of streets and narrow alleys.

As evening spread over the city, Judas returned to the Temple precincts. At the base of the south foundation wall several small fires were burning. He approached a man tending one of them.

"Peace," Judas said. "Tell me, may I sleep beside your fire tonight? I've no place to stay, as I'm a stranger to Jerusalem."

"Peace," the man replied. "Sure, you can lay your head down here. There's room."

Before he slept, Judas recalled his pleasant day, and then: *Tomorrow morning I'll go first thing to Simon. Hopefully, he'll have work for me.*

CHAPTER 16

The Alley of Red Lanterns.

Greeting Judas well before midday pleased Simon. He began by stating, "It's important you understand that a city like Jerusalem thrives because of its clever men. All great cities do."

Judas replied, "I really like Jerusalem. . . ."

"Good that you do. However, the question for me, my friend, is, are you a clever man?"

Simon calling him his friend surprised and delighted Judas. "I can read and write. I can sum. I'm comfortable handling money. I can haggle, which I did plenty of to keep Jesus and his friends fed and clothed."

"Ah, all necessary skills if you wish to work for me. But tell me, Judas, what do you really wish to achieve in Jerusalem?"

"I want to work for you and possibly get married here."

Simon, in a reflective mood, sat back in his chair. He doubted Judas would ever have long-term value to him, but, for the time being, he'd keep an open mind.

"How old are you Judas?"

"According to my mother, I think I must be twenty-four now."

Simon shifted his weight in the chair, considering what question should come next. "So you want to get married," he finally said.

"At some point. Jesus thought I should."

"Ah, your friend Jesus. Does he have any suggestions how you should go about that?"

"No, he just warns against certain things."

"Like what?"

"Adultery, fornication. . . ."

"What does he teach?"

"That it's sinful. He once said if a man so much as looks at a woman with lust in his heart, he commits the sin of adultery."

Simon laughed. "That's utter nonsense! Moses taught we should not commit the *act* of adultery. Good heaven, if what your Jesus teaches is true, every man in Jerusalem is doomed to Hell. Besides, for you to have relations with an unmarried girl would not be adultery. That is called fornication, an act not condemned by Moses."

"Jesus condemned it."

"Oh, so your Jesus is a better law giver than Moses? Is that what you're suggesting?"

"No, no. . . ."

"And from whom did Moses get the Law? From God himself, Judas! God himself. Think of that!"

Incapable of countering Simon, Judas said, "It's just that Jesus is so convincing when he teaches."

"Beware of smooth talkers, Judas. They can muddle your thinking."

At this point, Judas's thinking, without self-awareness, had been thoroughly muddled by Simon who now unexpectedly asked, "Tell me, do you ever think of sleeping with a woman?"

Surprised and somewhat shamed by the question, Judas admitted, "All the time."

"Just like all healthy, young men. Nothing for you, especially in your innocence, to be ashamed of. The lust inclination is inherent in the hearts of all men—young and old. It's our nature."

"Yes."

"And who gave us our human nature?"

Judas thought for a moment. "God, I guess."

"Exactly! It's the way God created men. Tell me, Judas, have you ever slept with a woman?"

Feeling a senseless humiliation, he answered, "No, I haven't"

At that honest revelation, Simon's expression became serious. He said nothing. Judas wondered what Simon might be thinking, causing him to feel even more demeaned. Wanting to change the topic he asked, "Can I work for you for money?"

Taken aback by the impudence of the question, Simon

answered, "Perhaps you can, Judas. Yes, perhaps, one day you can. But before we discuss that, is it true that you have never known the pleasures of a woman's body?"

"I never have, but I've dreamed about it."

Simon chuckled. "You're too old to be dreaming about it, Judas. You should have experienced it by now."

The broker pulled a coin from a purse girdled at his waist. He held it for Judas to gaze upon.

"This is Roman silver. It can purchase much of whatever a person might want. What would you like to purchase with it, Judas?"

"I don't know."

"There's a house in Jerusalem where you could spend the night with a beautiful young woman. For this single coin you could do with her whatever you desire."

"I don't have such a coin."

Simon stood and handed the coin to an astonished Judas. At his table, Simon wrote on a piece of papyrus. Turning toward Judas, he said, "Tonight, take the coin to this house in the Old City. Show what I have written to men on the street. They will direct you.

"I promise you, Judas, if you give the mistress of the house that coin, you will have a beautiful woman to sleep with. Then come back here tomorrow, and we'll talk about you working for me."

Judas could not fully appreciate this unexpected good fortune. After only two days in the Holy City he had made, he believed, a somewhat favorable impression on an influential man. And, incredibly, with a powerful coin now in his possession, he would at long last experience the deep, dark pleasures of a woman's body, a beautiful woman, just as Simon promised. And how could he doubt Simon? Simon called him his friend. Except for a well-deserved scolding about Judas's drunkenness at the supper of the Arimathean, the information broker treated Judas with more respect than he ever got from anyone except Jesus. Judas knew he could trust Simon, for how could he not trust a man who gave him a precious piece of Roman silver?

"Judas," Simon said, "when you leave here, go to a beard trimmer; have your hair trimmed as well. Then wash yourself. You don't want to enter the bed of a perfumed woman stinking like a stable. She might be a whore, but you don't want to repulse her."

"I don't have money for that."

Simon handed him several denarii after which Judas left. Simon smiled to himself thinking, *Young man, I suspect you just might prove a very profitable investment for me.*

Obeying the broker, Judas had his hair and beard trimmed. At a public cistern, he washed his face, neck, forearms, feet and lower legs. As he did so, he felt a smug satisfaction at having made a friend in the obviously wealthy Simon, for, he well understood, *a poor man can't give away Roman silver.* He also felt growing excitement in the realization of soon being with a woman.

Again he ate well by the wily skill of his hands. The evening though seemed to stretch itself out, allowing Judas to grow more anxious, restless, and edgy. The thought of being with a woman both thrilled and terrified him. He didn't know what to expect. Judas was profoundly aware of his lack of experience and wondered if the woman would ridicule him for it. That he could not bear.

Finally, in the black night, Judas descended into the poorest ghetto of the city seeking Simon's house of promised, sensual pleasures. He had to ask only two men to find its alley. He didn't know what the dark secrets of a young woman's body were, but now he was determined to discover them.

And then young Judas Iscariot—his breath rapid and shallow, heart pounding wildly against the cage of his chest, his mind and viscera overwhelmed by an unrelenting, adolescent lust—vanished into the maze of shadowy doorways and passages that configured the most notorious back alley of the old City of David, the alley of red lanterns.

Simon's powerful coin promised Judas a night encircled within the arms and legs of a beautiful woman. And yet, after less than an hour in which his awkwardness and inexperience led to disillusionment and disgust, he left this home for harlots. He grunted at the older woman who first welcomed him so pleasantly. In his mind, he cursed her and all the house inhabitants. He was angry and ashamed—ashamed of his clumsiness, his ignorance, his naiveté, even his fear in facing a young, smiling, half-naked girl, for in his inept immaturity, he allowed the sex act to become something crude and cruel.

He hurried down the alley. From within the shadow of a wall, a stooped beggar woman stepped in front of Judas. "Sir, a coin or two for an old widow…."

"Get out of my way you miserable hag."

As Judas passed around her, she reached feebly for his cloak.

He screamed, "Don't touch me, you filthy whore!"

Then, with the sharp edge of his palm, he struck hard at her junction of shoulder and neck. She shrieked in pain, but the sound was weak and pitiful. Only Judas heard it.

As she collapsed onto the damp alley stones, Judas rushed away. Her brittle collar bone had been shattered. She would suffer in agony the few remaining hours of her life and then die right before the long, width of dawn rose above the eastern hills.

CHAPTER 17

A walk from Jericho to Bethany.

Mary of Nazareth decided late to go to Jerusalem for Passover. Travelers from the south brought news that her son, Jesus, would be there. It had been months since Mary had seen him, and yet she had misgivings about making the long journey. Now nearing fifty years of age, diminishing strength and stamina concerned her. Legs, not fresh and sprightly as when young, troubled her most. She suspected she might have difficulty keeping up with whatever caravan she joined. While she didn't fear being left behind, she hoped other elderly women would also make the pilgrimage and be content to travel at a slower pace.

In Capernaum, Magdalene also learned that Jesus would be in Jerusalem for the festival. With a constant cue to herself to control her emotions, she longed to see Jesus again. She joined a group of pilgrims that set out for the Holy City, hoping to arrive there the third or fourth day of the week.

Deeply tired, Mary reached Jericho late Wednesday

afternoon. She immediately sought a place of rest. A while later, Magdalene arrived. She, too, needed rest. Once refreshed, however, both women enjoyed the pleasant city, for despite its desert location northeast of Jerusalem, Jericho, amid vast groves of palm and balsam trees, flourished in its perennial spring-like weather.

That evening, Magdalene spotted her Nazarene friend at a small market. The women were delighted to see each other and happy to learn they were going to Jerusalem for the same reason.

"Tomorrow, then, we'll reach the city" Magdalene said.

"I won't be able to," Mary said. "It's too much for me in one day."

"I had hoped to be there by Thursday."

"I'm planning to spend tomorrow night with some friends in Bethany. They are very welcoming. You could stay too."

Magdalene considered Mary's offer, which meant they'd arrive in Jerusalem on Friday. Passover week wouldn't end until the following Sabbath. Magdalene realized there would be time to encounter Jesus, probably on several occasions. "All right then," she said. "But Friday, I want to leave early so we get there at a reasonable hour."

"We will," Mary said.

After a good night's sleep and morning meal, Mary and Magdalene joined a group of fifteen heading for

Jerusalem. As they had agreed the evening before, they'd stop at the house of Lazarus and his two sisters and sleep there before completing their journey to Jerusalem.

From the mountain of the Holy City, the valley of Wadi Qelt flowed down and northward toward Jericho. This passage was the main and only trade route between the two cities. Though in places steep, narrow, rocky, and often plagued by bandits, the road to Jericho was well traveled. Pilgrims from Galilee and Capernaum walked it as the final stretch across the Jordan Valley and Judean Desert.

With walking sticks and full water bags, the two women began the slow, arduous climb toward the mountain of Jerusalem. On steep slopes they did not speak; on more gentle inclines they conversed.

"When Jesus was a youngster, we'd go every year for Passover," Mary said. "But after Joseph died, I was reluctant to make the journey, though Jesus did."

"I regret I didn't know your Joseph. What did he do?"

"He was a carpenter. He taught Jesus that trade."

"Did Jesus work as a carpenter?"

"For many years. . . . He even trained an apprentice. When Jesus left to begin his public life, he gave that young man all his tools."

"Were you surprised that he became a teacher?" Magdalene asked.

"Well, yes and no. When he was twelve there was an incident in Jerusalem that I didn't fully understand until Jesus began his ministry."

"What was that?"

"After festival week, we left Jerusalem thinking Jesus was with us, but he was not. We had already traveled a day when we realized he wasn't in our caravan. You can only imagine our concern. Anxiously, we returned to Jerusalem, but didn't find him until the third day."

"Where was he?"

"In the Temple, sitting in the midst of scholars and scribes, discussing scripture with them, as though he was their equal. We scolded him for failing to come with us. But he said, *Did you not know that I must be about my father's business?*[1]

"Then Joseph said, 'your father's business is carpentry.' When the scholars heard it they were aghast. One of them came to me and said, 'you must allow your son to stay and study with us. With instruction he will become a preeminent scholar, perhaps the finest Israel has ever known.'

"I shook my head. We would not allow that. Joseph beckoned Jesus to come, which he did, and we returned to Nazareth."

Magdalene said, "When Jesus talked about his father's business, he wasn't referring to Joseph, was he?"

---

1 Luke 2:49

"Of course not. He was referring to God, our heavenly Father. At the time, I truly did understand that, but he was just a boy. We wanted him with us, in our care. And, Magdalene, Jesus studied scripture all those years he was growing up. On his own he became a true scholar. Not a Temple scholar, but his knowledge seemed limitless, at least to me."

"So when he left to begin his public ministry, you well knew that he set out to do God's work," Magdalene said.

"Yes, of course. In my heart I knew he must do whatever God called him to do."

As the road steepened, the women ceased conversing. Mary's stride shortened and slowed, her breathing quickened. She struggled to climb some of the more difficult slopes.

Magdalene asked, "Are you all right? Should we stop and rest for a while?"

"No, I can make it."

When they reached a gentler incline Magdalene said, "You do know, Mary, that your son is more than a teacher."

"What can you tell me?"

"There's a small garrison of Roman soldiers in Capernaum. They guard the customs house and keep their eyes on Zealots. The captain, a centurion, is well-known by everyone in Capernaum. He's a good man; several years ago he actually built us a new synagogue. Jesus often teaches there.

"Well, this captain started coming to listen to Jesus. After several occasions, he began bringing other Roman soldiers. Needless to say, we were quite surprised by their presence."

"I would think so," Mary said. "After all, they don't believe in Yahweh."

"No, but our centurion had a servant who fell ill, almost to the point of death. When Jesus learned of it, he went to the centurion's house followed by a crowd of nosey neighbors, including me. When he saw Jesus approaching, he went to greet him. He said, *Lord, I am not worthy that you should enter under my roof, but only say the word and my servant shall be healed.*"[2]

"It's remarkable," Mary said, "that a Roman, a centurion no less, would so address a Jew; I mean with such humility."

"Yes, quite remarkable, unless he understands who Jesus truly is."

"Perhaps, but what happened then?" Mary asked.

"Jesus ignored his words, passing right by the captain into the house. The door closed and stayed closed while we waited, wondering what might be happening. After some time the captain came out and told us that Jesus said we should all go home. He intended to sup with the captain's family."

---

2 Matthew 8:8

"What happened to the servant?" Mary asked.

"We didn't know until the next day when I saw him at market. I asked him what happened; he answered that Jesus healed him."

"Oh, how wonderful," Mary said.

"From then on he, too, came to hear Jesus teach. All the Roman soldiers came. It was quite a sight—Jews and Gentiles listening to the beautiful words of your son."

"I suspect most Jews fear the Romans, or at least are wary of them."

"Not in Capernaum. Our town lives peaceably with the Romans. They're friendly; they treat us courteously, with respect, and all because of Jesus' teachings."

"Hmm," Mary smiled.

"Your son is a healer. Healers come from God. That servant wasn't the only one. I've heard other stories. Jesus is a prophet, a true prophet. You must believe me!"

Mary merely smiled. She knew.

Again steeper slopes stilled their conversation. After a day's walk they spotted, in the distance, shapes of a small village.

"Look, Magdalene," Mary said. "Bethany!"

CHAPTER 18

Pontius Pilate enters Jerusalem.

After his first sordid experience in a house of prostitution, Judas decided against returning to Simon's stall next morning, though he well knew the broker would be expecting him. Instead, he wandered about the Upper City where he sensed an undertone of anticipation and excitement. Gathering crowds seemed to be expecting something, so Judas finally asked.

"Our beloved Roman Governor is coming," a man sneered. "Pontius Pilate—hated by every Jew in this city."

Judas, unschooled in the not so subtle politics of Israel's relationship to Rome, asked, "Why?"

The man looked at him in disbelief. "Why? You mean you don't know? What are you—stupid?" He turned and walked away.

Judas loathed that word. It brought back wretched memories of his youth in Kerioth and how he left his birth place because of the general opinion of townsfolk that Judas was, indeed, a stupid, unkempt, foul-smelling boy. Now anger entered his heart and hatred his mind for any man who would dare call him stupid again. Besides, the Romans never hounded him. Until he got to Jerusalem he never encountered them. If anyone, it was Herod Antipas, murderer of John, the baptizer, whom he sensed he should fear and hate.

The governor of Idumaea, Judea and Samaria, entered sun-bright Jerusalem at the head of a long column of glinting imperial cavalry and infantry. Pilate lived in Caesarea by the sea, but with crowds of devout Jews flowing into Jerusalem to commemorate their liberation from Egypt, the Roman Governor put on a display of force to deter his Jewish subjects from getting too excited about the possibility of liberation from Rome. Pilate's procession was a manifestation of Roman imperialism. Every year, during Passover week, Pilate moved his headquarters to Jerusalem in a show of strength calculated to prevent any outbreaks of insurgency or violent rebellion against Roman rule. Such outbreaks were a constant threat because Rome imposed severe hardship on the lands of Palestine. Not even simple country folk want to cower beneath the heels of foreigners.

Pilate's entry into Jerusalem included horse mounted cavalry, helmeted foot soldiers in fine leather armor, weapons, banners, and imperial golden eagles mounted high on poles. Sights and sounds of the Roman procession had a powerful effect on all who witnessed it, especially young Judas. However, there were no welcoming cheers or shouts, as the proud governor rode past on a magnificent Arabian stallion, wanting merely to strike fear into the hearts and minds of Rome's bitter subjects.

Overwhelmed by this parade of power and might, yet favorably impressed, Judas had never seen anything like it. Even though the expressions on the Roman faces were grim and cruel, and even though he had been told that all of Jerusalem's Jews hated them, Judas enjoyed the Imperial spectacle with youthful enthusiasm.

As he trailed behind Pilate and his convoy, he noticed street vendors, just like the gawking crowds, seemed more interested in casting silent hatred for Rome through their timid eyes. As the governor rode past, men spit at their feet imagining the face of Pilate groveling in the dust below.

But for Judas, provided with more pleasure than hatred by the imposing procession, opportunities arose. That he could move unobtrusively along with the crowd was a natural talent. When he spotted several vendors focused on the passing Romans, Judas moved easily into position to swipe some delectable treats, even a piece of dried, salted fish that he would relish on the Temple steps.

After his pockets held his next meal, and as the Romans approached Pilate's palace, he experienced something new, a feeling that gave him great satisfaction. A smugness had entered his heart, titillating his mind. *What stupid fools those people in Kerioth are*, he thought. *Here I am, in the most important city in all of Palestine, watching the greatest military power in the world, my pockets stuffed with good food for which I paid not a single denarius. And they thought I was stupid. None of them have ever been to Jerusalem. None of them have ever seen the glory of Rome. But I can read and write, so if Simon gives me work, I will make money here. I'll get myself a house and wife and if not a wife then a woman. She'll cook for me, wash my clothes, and scrub my back.* At the thought of it, Judas laughed. *And she'll do whatever I want in bed. She'll be my obedient slave, and she'll kiss my feet for it.*

Realizing the afternoon light would soon fade, he decided to head back to the base of the Temple precincts where he ate and slept. Other men gathered there with whom Judas occasionally spoke. The crowds on both sides of the street were dispersing, people moving in all different directions. A beam of sunlight struck a group across the road. Judas saw, but could not believe, yet convinced himself somehow that it was the same girl, or was she a young woman, he had spotted in the marketplace yesterday. Again, he felt she was staring at him until their eyes met and she turned away.

Now Judas crossed the street, but with some difficulty, as many people moved in the opposite direction. When he got to the exact place, or so he thought, where she had been standing, she was nowhere to be seen, though several robed females scurried away. *Was it the same girl,* he wondered. *If so, why was she looking at me? And if she was, why would she run away?* It puzzled Judas, but he felt strangely flattered.

Early Wednesday, he returned to Simon's place in the Temple courtyard.

"Why didn't you come yesterday? I waited for you."

"I didn't feel right," Judas said.

"How'd it go at the house I sent you to? Did you get your money's worth?"

"Not so good. I was nervous."

"That's not unusual for a virgin. The second time will be better."

"I'd like to try it again."

"Don't be too anxious, Judas."

"Why not? I am anxious."

"Because you don't have money. I'm not going to finance your whoring."

At that, Judas slipped into a sullen silence.

Noticing it, Simon asked, "What did you do yesterday?"

"Not much, wandered around the Upper City. But then I saw the Roman governor enter Jerusalem. I was very impressed."

"Impressed by that scoundrel? Shame on you Judas. Don't you know he's hated by every Jew in this city?"

"Yes, I know. I'm not that stupid."

"Of course you're not! To prove it, can you recall what I told you is the most valuable thing in Jerusalem?"

Relieved he remembered, Judas said, "Information, but I'm not sure how that works."

"In fact, Judas, on the basis of information I suspect you have, or will soon have, you might be on the brink of working for us."

"Us? I don't understand," Judas said. "I thought I was to work for you."

"Let me ask you a question: Where is your friend, Jesus, right now?"

"I don't know. I haven't seen him since the Arimathean's dinner."

"Friday, most in Jerusalem will be sharing the Passover meal. Let me ask you this: Will you be sharing it with him?"

"Not Friday. Jesus told us Thursday. Yes, I'm supposed to; all twelve of us are. . . ."

"Why Thursday," Simon asked, surprised that he could learn that odd fact so easily. "And where will you eat?"

"I don't know, somewhere in Jerusalem," Judas answered. "Jesus told me that Thursday afternoon I should remain in the Temple precincts. One or two of the eleven will come fetch me."

"Then what?"

"Then we'll go someplace to share the Passover meal."

Simon fell silent. Judas sensed the broker was thinking what question he should ask next. But what Simon then said surprised Judas. "Would you like to sup with me and one of my associates this evening?"

Judas could hardly believe the invitation. He had been in Jerusalem not four days, yet now he was to dine with this influential man and his associate. He could scarcely imagine his good fortune. Again he thought of former Kerioth townsfolk. Now how stupid would they find him? In the heart of this great city he had been invited by the wealthy Simon, an information broker, keeper of a stall only steps from the holiest Temple in all of Israel, to dine with him and another important man.

"I'd like that very much."

"We'll treat you to one of Jerusalem's finest inns. Then afterward, if you've behaved well enough and not gotten drunk, I might be willing to slip you another Roman silver. You might desire a little pleasure before getting a good night's sleep." He grinned at Judas.

Deep within his abdomen, Judas felt again the strong stirring of his aching lust. A visceral desire overcame him. He wanted to experience the ecstatic pleasure offered by the body of a willing woman—he cared not at all that she was a prostitute—and he wanted it often.

There was a soft knocking on the jamb of the side portal. Simon glanced that way. When he saw who it was he said, "Oh, Joanna, come in."

An attractive, comely young woman entered. Glancing at Judas, she said, "Peace."

Judas bolted from his chair. Nearly shouting, all he could utter was, "You?"

CHAPTER 19

A trap is set.

"We'll be dining with my associate, Samuel. He's a prominent member of the Sanhedrin. As much as you enjoyed the Armiathean's dinner, Judas, this evening you will have the best meal of your life. I'm taking you to one of Jerusalem's finest inns."

The three men were led to a small, corner room that ensured privacy. After introductions and obligatory greetings of *Peace,* Samuel said, "I understand you'd like to work for us."

Again the word *us* surprised Judas. "I had wanted to work for Simon."

"Samuel is a close partner, so to speak. On occasion we're involved in various matters where we have common interests."

"So Judas, have you enjoyed getting to know Jerusalem?" Samuel asked, pleasantly.

"Very much," Judas answered. "I like it here."

"What have you done; what have you all seen?"

"I enjoy the Upper City. I look at all the great houses and palaces. Yesterday I saw the Roman governor enter the city. That really impressed me."

"You might be impressed," Samuel began, "but it's important to understand that Pilate holds the fate of Jerusalem in his hands, or should I say in his Legions? The Romans are invaders, occupiers of what is not theirs, and they hold the power of life and death over every Jew in Jerusalem. I would advise you not to be impressed by them. Better you fear them."

Judas did not respond.

The dinner, however, did prove, to Judas's limited experience, to be the best meal he ever had. He observed how slowly his companions ate and drank, so he imitated them. While he might have had, at times, a tendency to gulp his wine, he restrained himself, aware that he did not want to make an unfavorable impression on Samuel. He knew Simon expected that of him.

"You have a good appetite," Samuel said.

Judas smiled at the man. "Yes, I do."

"But tell me, how do you eat when apart from Simon's generosity?"

"What do you mean?"

"How do you obtain food?"

"I pick up a little here and there."

"Did you have money left from the coin I gave you?" Simon asked.

"Yes, yes I did."

"Don't lie to us, Judas."

"I'm not lying."

"On Monday after you left me, yesterday, and earlier today, you stole from the markets."

"No," Judas protested.

"We have witnesses," Simon said.

Suddenly, Judas realized he was being attacked.

"After you left my stall Monday afternoon, we had persons who work for us follow you."

"Spies?"

"Yes, I suppose you can call them that."

"Why . . . why would you do that?"

"Because we needed to get to know you better, Judas. Especially, if you're going to work for us."

Now Judas felt a tightening, enclosing, demeaning fear, realizing that both Simon and Samuel knew he was a thief. "I had to eat. I had no money. I was hungry."

"So you stole from a poor baker, and the fish and fruit mongers. . . ."

"I only took a little. . . ."

"Your cloak is cleverly sewn, isn't it, Judas?"

"Why do you ask that?"

"Because when you put stolen goods into your cloak, it must have very deep pockets to hide it all."

"No. . . ."

"Show us your cloak," Samuel said.

"It's not true. My mother sewed my cloak. It's always been this way," Judas lied.

"Show us!" Samuel demanded.

Judas stood. He opened his cloak. The men laughed.

"Just as we suspected. Those pockets could hold enough to feed ten hungry men. Judas, you are a thief."

"Only when I'm hungry and have no money. I'm not a thief, at least not all the time."

"We followed you yesterday and earlier today while you strolled so casually through the markets, putting whatever delicacies caught your fancy into those oversized pockets. You are a thief, Judas. A reasonably skillful one at that, but let me tell you something . . . ," Simon paused.

"What?" Judas asked.

"As subtle and sly as your thievery is, we have many eyes in Jerusalem even more subtle, even more sly."

"But why spy on me?"

"We need to know what you really are," Simon said. "We needed to get information about you, so we could decide if we should hire you. We needed the kind of information such that, once in our possession, it would assure your willingness to work for us."

"But I am willing to work for you."

Samuel said, "Do you really think we'd hire a common thief? The only reason we're talking to you at all is because of the work you did for Jesus, your friendship with him. That makes you uncommon. We presume you did not steal from him. By the way, do you know what the Romans do with thieves?"

"No," Judas answered.

"They crucify them—you do know what crucifixion is?"

"Yes." The thought of the Roman death torture terrified Judas.

"Tell me, are you aware this coming Friday two thieves will be crucified by the Romans?"

"No."

"The Romans don't like thieves. They ruin the tranquility of a well-ordered city. These two men were stealing all the time. We Jews got tired of it. We jailed them, mentioned it to the governor, Pilate, and he wrote the death orders."

Terror seized Judas's entire being. He could not speak. He sat there wondering if he was understanding correctly what Samuel seemed to be implying.

Simon said, "Now do you understand the power of information, Judas? We know this about you, and were we to turn you over to the Romans, they'd be delighted to have a third thief to crucify."

Judas had considered Simon his friend, yet now he spoke like an enemy. His first sense of Simon's betrayal aroused his mind; now all became obvious: Simon feigned friendship while spying on Judas to learn his weaknesses. With that information he easily trapped Judas in a situation he could not extricate himself from. Suddenly, he exclaimed, "My God, it was Joanna who spied on me!"

"Perhaps," Simon said.

"Don't mention that woman's name again," Samuel said. "Not you who slept with a whore."

Surprised that Samuel knew, Judas said, "Simon suggested it."

"Well, it wasn't quite that simple, Judas. We discussed the difference between fornication and adultery, the Law of Moses. You told me what Jesus teaches, your youthful lack of sexual experience, and your desire to have a woman. I made a recommendation, gave you a coin were you to take the recommendation, but I did not command you to go to a house of prostitution. That was your decision, yours alone."

"What happened that night?" Samuel asked.

"Nothing. . . . It was a bad experience."

"Did you encounter anyone?"

"No."

"After you left the whore, what about that old beggar woman in the street?"

The question startled Judas. *How could he possibly know that?* "She was a nuisance."

"Why did you strike her?"

Judas found it almost unbelievable that they knew what had happened between the woman and himself. There was no one else in the alley. No one that he could see. But in the shadows eyes lurked, watching and following Judas. It was those eyes paid by Simon that had witnessed what would so easily become highly useful and powerful information.

"She grabbed my cloak. She was a filthy old hag."

"Even so, why did you strike her?"

"She touched me, wanted money. I was tired. I didn't want to deal with an old hag. I needed sleep."

"What happened after you struck her, Judas?" Simon asked.

"Nothing. What do you mean?"

"She screamed and fell onto the stones of the alley. You know that."

"I got out of there. I don't know what happened. I needed sleep."

"It's important that you understand something about encountering her, Judas."

"What?"

"That you killed her. She died before the light of day."

"That can't be. I didn't hit her that hard. I certainly didn't mean to kill her."

"Hard enough, Judas," Samuel said. "Unfortunately for you, she died—you killed her. That makes you, in addition to being a thief, a murderer."

"No," Judas protested; "I'm not a murderer."

"We have an eye witness who will testify that you killed her. We can even produce her corpse, if the Romans doubt us."

Simon said, "It is very important, Judas, that you understand the power of our information. We have witnesses to your thievery and you murdering that helpless, old woman. In fact, we have so much information that were we to present it to the Romans you would undoubtedly be crucified. So, don't even think of leaving Jerusalem. Our eyes will be on you now all the time. Were you to leave, we will send Roman soldiers to bring you back. If you leave, you will seal your fate. You will be crucified."

Trapped and caged like a wild animal, Judas felt it with the same intense bewilderment of a dumb creature. He felt it with a deep, visceral rage, felt it with a natural desire to be free and far away, and he felt it with an unbounded hatred for those two who so skillfully had set the trap. Judas looked at Simon and Samuel in disbelief, realizing he no longer controlled his own life, his own freedom, his destiny. They did. They controlled him as certainly and completely as though he were a chained, muzzled dog.

Suddenly, Judas recalled what Jesus had warned: *be on your guard for those who might seem your friend, but would just as soon lead you astray.* Surprisingly, Judas also recognized how stupid he was to have stolen John's water bag. He concluded that seeking Jesus was a terrible mistake. He should have gone straight to Jerusalem even if it meant having to clear the streets and alleys of animal dung, garbage and rats.

The entire essence of Judas Iscariot's being now realized he was captive within an invisible cube of closely spaced iron bars from which he could never escape. Though, he presumed, he was still free to roam the streets and alleys of Jerusalem, and even free to continue stealing from the food mongers, he could not leave the walled city, for to do so would assure his crucifixion. That thought terrified him nearly to the edge of madness. It showed in his face and a trembling of his hands.

"What can I do?" he finally asked.

"You must work for us," Samuel said. "You must do exactly what Simon tells you to do, and I have every reason to believe you will. You understand clearly now that if you don't, we will hand you over to the Romans."

With no idea what work they intended for him, Judas replied, "Yes, of course I will. You don't have to threaten me. I'll do whatever you want."

Simon patted Judas's arm. "Don't worry about any of this. You will be surprised how easy your task is. And you'll be well paid.

"We don't mean to threaten you, Judas. We just want you to know how the Romans treat law breakers. You have to understand how things really work here in Jerusalem. The Romans do not like murderers or thieves. Therefore, you have to give up your thievery if you want to live."

"But if I have no money, I have to eat."

"While you work for us, Judas, you will have money. You won't have to steal anymore. Thievery is too dangerous a business. Sooner or later you'll be caught."

In spite of that warning, Judas said, "I still have to eat."

Simon opened his purse, withdrew a coin, and handed it to Judas. "No more stealing. You're important to us now. We can't afford to have you steal, be caught, then crucified in two days. We deal with more important matters than your petty thievery."

Samuel rose from the table. "I'm tired; I have to leave. Simon you know what to do. Goodnight to you both."

After the bill was settled, Simon and Judas left the inn.

"Come to my stall tomorrow, mid-morning. I'll instruct you on your first assignment."

"Samuel frightens me. Why does he have to do that?"

"Oh, I know he can be rather harsh with a new informant, but he really only wants to assure that you'll be loyal in your dealings with us. We need to know that you'll do exactly what we tell you to do. We have to have confidence in you, Judas. Surely you can understand that."

"Can you tell me what the work involves?"

"Only this: it has to do with information—what else—for which you will be paid handsomely."

"What information of mine can be of any possible value to you?"

"We'll discuss it in the morning."

For several strides they did not speak until Judas said, "One other thing: who is Joanna? Could I meet her?"

"I don't want you ever mentioning her name again."

"Why not?"

"Because she's of a higher social standing. She's virtuous, pure. You went whoring."

"You encouraged me to."

"No, I didn't."

The denial dumbfounded Judas Iscariot, who was not so stupid as to not know when he was being lied to.

"But Simon, you gave me the number of the house. You wrote it down."

"I don't remember that. Show me."

Judas searched his pockets, but the parchment scrap was gone. He did not recall throwing it away.

"I swear you gave it to me."

Simon said, "Well, I swear I did not encourage you to go whoring. That was your decision, not mine."

Confused by Simon's denial of what was so obvious, Judas said nothing. He knew it was the information broker who gave him Roman Silver to pay for his pleasure. He knew the broker wrote the house number for Judas to seek and find. He knew Simon encouraged Judas's youthful lust. What he didn't know was why Simon now would deny it. If any good came out of this, it was that Judas learned the devious duplicity of a man he thought he could trust.

"Would you at least tell me who Joanna is?"

"I see no reason to tell you. Under no circumstances will I allow you to approach her."

"Please, just tell me who she is. I saw her spying on me. I'd like to know."

Unsurprised at Judas's thick-headedness in his inability to deduce the obvious, and in a moment of careless exasperation, Simon said, "She's my daughter, you idiot!"

CHAPTER 20

An unexpected visit.

In spite of a good night's sleep in the same bed her son, Jesus, had slept in only two nights prior, Mary woke feeling tired and ill. She realized, as she had previously, that traveling demanded too much of her.

At the morning meal, she told Magdalene she couldn't possibly make the final trek to Jerusalem that day.

"Mary, we agreed yesterday we wouldn't leave until early tomorrow. Did you forget?"

"Oh, that's right. Yes, I must have. . . ."

The day broke sunny and mild, not as warm as the weather in Jericho, but probably not as cool as the mountain top of Jerusalem either. The four women enjoyed each other's company, though Mary excused herself midmorning to rest and then later in the day to nap. With all her heart, she wanted to travel to the Holy City the following morning, longed to see her son and, hopefully, share Passover with him that evening.

"We wanted Jesus to stay with us this entire week and share our Passover," Martha said.

"You know he wanted to be in Jerusalem," Lazarus said.

"Bethany is a far quieter, safer, cleaner place," Martha said.

"That's of little concern to Jesus," Mary, sister of Lazarus, said. "I've never known any man so confident, so sure of himself."

"And fearless," Magdalene added. "I saw that in Capernaum."

"Strong, too," Mary said. "He worked hard as a carpenter. I know my son. His body is all muscle."

Hearing voices approaching, they turned toward the front gate.

Lazarus went to look. "My heaven, it's the brothers Peter and Andrew." Greeting them, he asked, "What brings you here?"

"Jesus sent us to find his mother." Spotting her, Peter said, "Peace Mary, and to you, too, Magdalene."

Martha asked, "Would you like something to eat?"

"No, Martha, we have to return to Jerusalem," Andrew said. "Jesus wishes to celebrate his Passover supper this evening."

"That's strange," Jesus' mother said. "He knows the traditional meal is Friday."

"Ah, but who are we to question the Master," Peter said.

"Well, now that you know I'm here," Mary said, "did Jesus have a message for me?"

"Yes, he wants you to come, so you can share supper with him, with all of us."

"I can't possibly," Mary said. "I need another good night's sleep. Tomorrow Magdalene and I will come."

"He'll be disappointed."

"He'll understand."

"Did Jesus mention my name?" Magdalene asked.

The question surprised Peter. "No, why would he?"

Hearing Peter's casual indifference, Magdalene hid a piercing pain, so obvious in her eyes, deep in her heart.

The brothers started to leave, but then turned back to face the small group.

"There's something I think you should know," Peter began. "Last Monday morning, Jesus caused a ruckus in the Temple precincts."

"What?" they all exclaimed.

"Jesus doesn't cause ruckuses," Lazarus said.

"He did Monday," Peter said. "He drove the money changers and dove sellers, all the merchants, from the Temple. It was a mess with money from the changers' tables spilling all over, and hundreds of people scrambling to steal as much of it as they could. It was terrible for us to witness. We expected Jesus to be arrested, but nothing happened. The Jewish guards seemed too afraid to rise against him, and the Romans never came."

Andrew said, "When he walked away, untouched, the crowd parted like Moses parted the sea. You could just sense the great respect they had for his authority and power."

"Is it safe for Jesus in Jerusalem?" his mother asked.

"I think so," Peter said. "Many of his followers are there."

Andrew said, "Peter, we have to go back now. We have to find Judas."

CHAPTER 21

Judas's assignment.

After dining with Simon and Samuel, Judas could not sleep. He felt cold to the point of shivering, though the night air was mild. The horror of contemplating his own crucifixion obsessed his mind and overwhelmed his terrified heart. He was powerless to dispel either the thought or the feeling. He double wrapped his cloak around himself to no avail. Thus, he did not sleep during the long night, for his restless, chilled body was saturated with fear.

At dawn, Judas rose. He was thirsty, but not hungry, for he had eaten well the evening before. Now, as the eastern sky lightened, he was far too distracted to concern himself with the needs of his belly. He went straight to Simon's stall. Though feeling wretched, he paced in front of it until Simon arrived.

"You're early," Simon said.

"I couldn't sleep."

"Are you so anxious to learn your little task?" Simon spoke pleasantly, unlike the night before when he denied complicity in Judas's visit to a prostitute. The question put Judas more at ease.

"Yes."

"Then tell me, Judas: this evening are you still planning to share Passover with your Jesus?"

"I think so. Nobody's told me otherwise."

Simon leaned back in his chair, folding his hands in front of his lips. For several moments he did not speak, nor did Judas.

"Judas, sit down." He motioned with a pointed finger. "What we need you to do is quite simple. You must identify Jesus for us. That shouldn't be too difficult, should it?"

"But why? You've seen him. You know what he looks like."

"Right now there're thousands of Galilean men in Jerusalem all with long hair and scruffy beards, just like Jesus and his friends and you, too, before you went to the trimmer."

"I'm not Galilean. I'm Judean."

"Oh that's right—I forgot. Well, in any event, Jesus is one of those thousands. They all look pretty much the same to me."

"What exactly do you want me to do?"

"I want you to positively identify Jesus, so there's absolutely no doubt in anyone's mind."

"How?"

"Before we discuss that, you should know the reason

we're ordering you to do this. There are some very import-ant, powerful people in Jerusalem who want to meet your Jesus, who want to talk to him, learn his teachings. I know and you know that Jesus would not accept an invitation to talk with any of those people."

"Who do you mean?" Judas asked.

"The high priests, chief priests, the most important members of the Sanhedrin, the most respected magis-trates. . . ."

"Why didn't they engage him when he taught in the Temple?"

"That's irrelevant now, and besides, you're not one to question me. Have you forgotten what we discussed last evening with Samuel? Have you forgotten that we control whether you live or die? So, no more questions. The fact is you have no say in any of this. What we expect you to do is figure out, with my help of course, when and where you can positively identify Jesus. This is your first task; for it you will be paid well."

Judas hesitated, but could not control his curiosity. "How well?"

"Thirty pieces of Roman silver." Simon stared hard at Judas; he detected in Judas's expression pleasure at hearing the amount. In his own mind, Simon relished contemplat-ing seventy, easy Roman silvers for himself.

"Let me ask you this," Simon began. "After you finish your supper where do you think Jesus might go?"

"I don't know," Judas answered. "Maybe the Temple."

"When will you find out? Can you find out?"

"I suppose so. They'll talk about it. At some point I'll know."

"As soon as you definitely know, you are to come here. I'll be waiting."

"Then what?"

"Then we'll arrange to encounter Jesus, so you can positively identify him."

"Should I point; should I touch him; what exactly should I do?"

Again Simon leaned back in his chair, thinking what might be an unmistakable sign. Then it came to him.

"A kiss, Judas. Kiss him on his cheek."

CHAPTER 22

Simon's bewilderment.

He waited, as instructed, on the arched causeway linking the Temple precincts to the Upper City. Late in the afternoon, Peter and Andrew approached. "Peace Judas. We're glad we found you."

The three men hurried through the wealthy district to a building opposite the house of Joseph of Arimethea, which Judas acknowledged by pointing.

"The Arimethean owns this, too," Peter said. "He's a very rich man."

Jesus and nine others were already gathered in the large, upper room, well-furnished for the Passover supper. To Judas he said, "We haven't seen you for a while. I suppose you know Jerusalem better now than you did when we last dined with Joseph."

"Yes, I do," Judas said, somewhat awkwardly. A deceitful shame smeared his mind.

"Well, I'm glad you came tonight. Important that we all be together."

At that, in a swift, piercing thought, Judas realized the

simple task he had to complete in a coming hour of darkness to save his own life. Without thinking, he blurted, "I still want to work here and find a wife."

Not responding, Jesus turned abruptly from Judas, engaging others in conversation.

The same young women who served at Joseph's table, now brought in food and wine for the Passover meal.

As they all began to recline, Judas asked Peter, "What does Jesus intend after supper?"

"We're going to Gethsemane, probably spend the night in the garden there."

Surprised, Judas said, "Why cross the Kidron? Why not stay in Jerusalem, stay here? It's warmer."

Peter looked dismissively at Judas. "Who are you to question what Jesus wishes to do?"

Judas ate without conversing, only a few softly spoken words exchanged with Jesus. Before the meal ended, that is, before Jesus broke again fresh bread and poured new wine, Judas withdrew from table and room with little notice.

Slipping out along the passageway, Judas descended the stairs and rushed through the darkening streets to Simon's stall in the shadows of the Temple courtyard. Greatly pleased to see Judas, Simon, too, was surprised that Jesus would go to Gethsemane.

"I think Jesus and the others plan to sleep there," Judas said.

"Sleep?" Simon said, incredulously. "Have you forgotten your task? We'll go to Gethsemane so you can identify Jesus, just as we've planned. There'll be no sleeping there tonight, I assure you."

"No, oh . . . , that's right. I forgot. For just a moment I forgot what I must do."

"Judas, stay alert now. Think of what we'll experience. Soon we'll see Jesus and his friends cross the courtyard. We'll see them pass this way, not knowing we're watching. They'll pass the night guards at the East Gate, but we'll wait a while before following. We'll give them time in the garden before we join them. When we do, as soon as you confront Jesus, kiss him. Then your work is done. This is going to be a very good night for us, Judas, and for it, you will earn a small fortune."

That unlikely word incited Judas's greed.

Smiling broadly in the faint lamp glow, Simon said, "Think of it Judas. After tonight you will be one of Jerusalem's richest vagabonds. Be happy, young man!"

Judas didn't know how to respond, so he simply feigned laughter. In fact, possessing a fair number of Roman silvers excited him, like lust.

Both men reclined comfortably, waiting for Jesus to pass eastward and for themselves to commence the coming events of this night in a dark, lonely garden.

After a long pause, Simon spoke. "You know, Judas, I've given a great deal of thought to your Jesus."

"How so?" Judas asked.

"Why would a man like that choose the kind of life he has? It seems so strange to me, so unconventional, that a man with a trade, whether he's a carpenter or vintner, would freely choose to wander throughout Palestine preaching some new, radical ideas.

"A normal Jew, living in a small provincial town in Galilee, would learn and master a trade such as Jesus did with carpentry. He'd get married to a girl he's known from childhood, have children, raise a family, attend synagogue, build tables and chairs and beds for the townspeople, help build a local wine press if asked, raise a roof when needed, watch his children grow, and then grow old and become an esteemed member of his little village. And he'd become, if so well-learned, as Jesus apparently is, an elder teacher in synagogue.

"But," Simon wondered aloud, "why did Jesus reject all of that to wander about a vast countryside teaching whatever it is he's teaching? Why abandon such a simple, comfortable life to wander like a nomad, never having enough food, rarely sleeping in a bed, wearing worn, shabby clothes and thin sandals? It makes no sense to me."

"I don't know," Judas said. "He just does."

"And why would a group of men, all with trades, make the decision to leave wives, children, and work to follow such a man? And to do it for several years now, as I understand it. It makes absolutely no sense to me, Judas. I just can't comprehend it." Simon spoke truly, his lack of insight authentic, genuine.

"I can't either."

"Why isn't he content with our ancient religion, the religion of his ancestors, for God's sake? Why doesn't he cherish our ancient ways, our God-given laws, the history and poetry of our scriptures? Surely he knows we worship the one, true God—Yahweh. What can Jesus possibly offer to improve on that?"

"Nothing, I guess," Judas said. "But he does love scripture. That I know from when he taught me to read."

"Well, tonight, he can explain himself to the high priests, maybe even the king."

"Who . . . what king?

"Herod Antipas."

"He's evil. He killed the baptizer . . . beheaded him. That's evil."

"Judas, watch what you say. That crazy baptizer publicly, loudly, and repeatedly slandered the king and queen. That's a capital offense. He got what he deserved. You be careful what you say, or he'll have your head, too."

Judas said nothing, but held his belief.

Simon spoke no more until, "I hear voices . . . someone's coming."

From the shadows they observed twelve men heading toward the East Gate.

"That's them," Judas exclaimed.

"Quiet. The air is still. They'll hear you."

They waited, speechless, until the small group moved farther away.

"Good," Simon said, "we'll wait now, give them time to get settled before we join them."

"Yes."

After a lengthy pause, Simon said, "Of course, you, too, made a decision to follow Jesus. How come?"

"I needed work, so he put me in charge of the purse. I did well for him, for them all. He taught me to read and write. That's why I can work in Jerusalem now."

"Judas, you need a purpose to succeed in Jerusalem, plus the necessary skills to achieve that purpose. You have none of that."

"Are you saying my reading and writing don't matter?"

"You haven't read enough to be considered even remotely educated. You can read and maybe write a little, but you're still basically a stupid man."

Simon's words slashed across Judas's heart, while old, wretched memories of Kerioth rose within.

"You really don't belong in Jerusalem nor, for that matter, does Jesus and that bunch of provincial fishermen who follow him. They don't belong in Jerusalem any more than you do."

Judas disagreed, at least regarding Jesus and himself. Simon was correct about the others; they all should have stayed in their small, distant towns. However, Judas's pride convinced him, in spite of Simon's opinion, that Jesus and he belonged in this wonderous city. After all, hadn't Jesus told him it was their *destiny*?

"You see, Judas, this is a very sophisticated city. The successful, powerful people here are well-educated, well-bred, and all well-connected. You might aspire to that, but you'll never attain it. You enjoy roaming about the Upper City, admiring the grand houses and wealth, but you will never belong there; you will never be accepted there. You, like all provincials of such low social rank, are incapable of mastering the complexities of society, politics, religion, and commerce, how they all blend together here in the life of Jerusalem. To do that, one must be born into Jerusalem's upper class, must be born to the right family, and properly educated."

Simon's somber assessment disheartened Judas. Now he felt the inferiority of his birth, of his background, his education, and he despised all of it.

"Don't be discouraged. You're not the only one who shouldn't be in Jerusalem. Jesus doesn't belong here either."

"He always comes for Passover."

"I know, but that doesn't mean he should. After what he did several days ago when he behaved like a madman causing all that havoc among the money changers and dove sellers, he should have been thrown into prison. That's what would have happened to anyone else. I still find it odd that he wasn't arrested. He made many enemies that day. Powerful people have long memories, Judas, that won't be forgotten or forgiven so soon. Too much stealing occurred because of your Jesus. The merchants were stolen from by the rabble, the very people who follow Jesus the most. God told Moses we are not to steal. I hope by now even you know that, or should. So how is your Jesus a man of God if he causes such immorality? Yes, I understand, the rich are not to steal from the poor, but it also works the other way: the poor are not to steal from the rich, and that is exactly what happened because of Jesus.

"But really, Judas, what good did it do? Next day it was almost business as usual, and the day after that. Your Jesus, of course, was nowhere to be seen. He comes and goes like a wind. A very odd man, in my opinion. Very odd indeed."

"I don't understand him completely, but he doesn't seem odd to me. And in spite of what you say, I still want to work and live in Jerusalem. I'll show you. I'll prove myself. I can obey orders. I still want to work for you."

"We'll see about that. Let's see how it goes tonight and what the morning brings."

"What do you mean?"

"I don't have any other work for you, Judas. Whether I will tomorrow or the day after remains to be seen. I just don't know. I can't promise you anything."

"Unless I work for you, I don't know what I could do in Jerusalem."

"You'd slave as a common laborer."

"I don't want that. I slaved on animal farms. Never again."

"Then you should leave. Go back to Kerioth."

"Never. I hate that town."

"Let me give you some advice, Judas. Forget your Jerusalem dreams. Go away from here. Find a quiet town, learn a trade, marry a simple girl and live a simple life."

"No, I will show you tonight that you can trust me. You must give me more work."

"Listen to me: right now I promise you nothing. We have to go." Simon rose, then Judas. "Your first task beckons. Do it well! Then we'll see."

At those confusing, contradictory words, despair, or was it a pebble of hope, sank into the well of Judas's heart. Had he been alone, had he not had a commission to fulfill to free himself from a certain Roman death, had he not the promise of money, despair would have prevailed.

Others also watched Jesus and the eleven, as they headed east. Samuel organized and instructed a Temple military guard as to their duty, which Simon and Judas now joined. With torches blazing, the entourage headed toward Gethsemane along the well-traveled path crossing the Kidron Valley. Judas's heart raced, though his mind was clear and focused. He knew a simple kiss on the cheek

of Jesus would liberate him from a fear and fate of crucifixion, favorably impress both Simon and Samuel, and
give him wealth far beyond the limit of his youthful greed.
Absorbed in these thoughts, he failed to notice that all the
soldiers bore arms.

CHAPTER 23

A fateful kiss.

In the moonless garden, the Temple guard led by Samuel and followed by Simon and Judas waited for Jesus and his friends to appear. Torch light drew them to encounter.

"Do the deed quickly," Simon whispered to Judas, while pushing lightly against his back.

With uncharacteristic boldness, Judas made straight for Jesus. "Hail Teacher," he said, before kissing him on his cheek.

Startled, Jesus said, "Judas, dost thou betray the Son of Man with a kiss?"[3]

"Betray? No Master, no!" The word horrified Judas. "Important men want to speak with you. They merely asked me to identify. . . ."

Then, with force, Simon pulled Judas back away from Jesus, while Samuel and the Temple guard captain confronted Jesus and arrested him.

---

3 Luke 22:48

"They're arresting him," Judas shouted. "There's no need. . . ."

"Quiet," Simon said. "It's a mere formality. You know very well Jesus wouldn't go willingly to speak with any of the authorities. They arrest only because it assures that Jesus will cooperate."

With hands bound, Jesus was led away in the midst of the Temple guard. His other eleven friends had fled.

"This is all wrong," Judas said. "He isn't a criminal."

"That's debatable, but not for us and certainly not now. Come, we'll follow them."

A satisfied Simon and a distraught Judas trailed closely behind the torch light of the Temple throng heading back toward Jerusalem.

After a while, Simon said, "He'll be taken to the most important, powerful men. Thanks to us, they'll have opportunity to question him about his teachings, his healings. That's what this night is all about, and you played an important role, Judas. These men truly want to understand his appeal, how it could attract so many followers. And for Jesus, he'll have several chances to clearly explain his teachings. In other words, what you and I did tonight was necessary to help the authorities of our great city understand what your Jesus is all about. Does that make sense to you?"

"I suppose so," Judas said, with little spirit.

"After all questionings are concluded, I'm sure Jesus will

be invited, perhaps by the High Priest himself, to spend the night in a palatial bed. Then, in the morning you can rejoin Jesus and the others, if any of those cowards return."

"Yes," Judas said.

"You did what we asked you to do. Here, you earned this."

Simon handed Judas a leather money bag with thirty pieces of promised Roman silver. "Now you have a fine money bag to go along with your fine water bag."

Judas clutched the bag of coins, forgetting for a moment the distress he felt at witnessing the arrest of Jesus. He realized he held more money in his hands than he had ever possessed before. He felt an odd exhilaration, like pride, and couldn't help recalling the poor, stupid people he left behind in Kerioth. *What would they think of me now?* he wondered.

Climbing toward the East Gate, Judas again expressed, though more calmly, his disappointment that they arrested Jesus. Again Simon assured him that was the only way they could get Jesus to give testimony.

Back at the Temple courtyard, Simon and Judas watched as the guarded Jesus crossed the arched causeway leading to the Upper City and the house of Annas, father-in-law of Caiphas, the High Priest that year.

"Judas, your Jesus will do himself well tonight. He'll converse in a civilized manner with civilized men. You mustn't think otherwise. You know how smart he is."

139

"Yes, he is."

"You should get some rest, too. Here. . . ." Simon slipped one more Roman silver onto Judas's palm along with some lesser coins. "Spend the night in the arms of your favorite woman. Have a night of pleasure and sleep. Don't fear for your Jesus."

"No, you're right, I should not. I know how strong he is."

The men, with equivalent contempt, slurred each other a good night. Judas turned away from the Temple to descend the Herodian staircase to the Lower City. In the darkness, he easily found his way to the old city of David and its secret alley of red lanterns. He knocked; the door opened slightly. Recognizing him, she smiled a whore's welcome. Instantly, a wild lust engulfed his reality.

CHAPTER 24

The road to Jerusalem.

"You've a fine morning to travel," Lazarus told Magdalene and Jesus' mother, as they prepared for their long walk to Jerusalem. Rested and fresh after two nights' good sleep, both women were anxious to get to the Holy City, excited and happy to once again be with Jesus. Each carried a water bag, a chunk of bread, some dried fruit, and a walking stick.

"Send our love to Jesus," Lazarus's younger sister said. "He's always welcome here."

"Yes," Martha agreed. "Tell him he should come visit us after he leaves Jerusalem."

"We will," Magdalene said.

"And tell him his friends are welcome, too, even Judas," Lazarus said.

Martha, glancing at her brother, grimaced. "I suppose. . . ."

Mary, the younger sister, said, "When you return to Capernaum stop and visit us again."

"We'll probably go straight to Jericho, but we could

stop for a little while," Magdalene said. "We won't spend the night though."

Returning to the oasis city was much faster and easier because the road sloped downward the entire way.

"Well, in any event, we look forward to seeing you soon," Lazarus said.

"Goodbye then," Jesus' mother said. "Keep us in your prayers."

Mary, Magdalene, and the siblings joined in gentle, farewell embraces.

The rising road to Jerusalem was circuitous, rendering their journey far longer than a bird's straight-line flight.

"Would you like to come with me to Capernaum?" Magdalene asked Mary. "Before you return to Nazareth, I mean."

"Yes, I think I'd enjoy that."

"Jesus likes our little town. He's taught in our synagogue often."

"Perhaps I should consider living there. I am getting older, you know."

"That would be wonderful. I'll introduce you to all my friends."

"Nazareth isn't so pleasant now, not like the old days."

"Why is that?" Magdalene asked.

"Because Jesus never comes to teach in our synagogue anymore."

"I'm surprised. . . ."

"Don't be! Several years ago he was reading scripture for our congregation. They didn't like his interpretation of a particular passage, in fact, it angered them. They thought him arrogant and boastful. Many of those townspeople knew Jesus their entire lives, since his boyhood. They regarded him merely as a carpenter or the son of a carpenter, not an authority of sacred scripture. Nevertheless, their anger was so great they drove him from our town. I thought they might harm him, but he fled safely."

"I'm shocked," Magdalene said. "We like it when he explains scripture. He makes it so clear. But, Mary, why doesn't he return at least to visit you?"

"Realize this, Magdalene: Jesus has shaken the dust of Nazareth from his sandals forever. He will never come back! That is why I'd be comfortable moving to Capernaum. Hopefully, I'll get to see my son more often there."

They ate and rested at the Mount of Olives, preparing to cross the Kidron Valley before climbing the winding path to the East Gate of the Temple Mount.

"Soon we'll be in Jerusalem," Magdalene said. "It's almost midday."

When they arrived at the vast Courtyard of the Gentiles, they found it deserted. They entered the sacred Temple to pray for several moments before discussing where they might find Jesus, as they both first expected to see him, along with a crowd, in the Temple precincts.

They decided to descend to the Lower City, asking everyone they encountered if they knew the whereabouts of Jesus, the Nazorean.

As they walked across the courtyard, they recognized a young man, one of the closest friends of Jesus, running toward the East Gate. Visibly disturbed to see them, he could barely respond to their greetings of "Peace."

"John, where are you rushing off to?" Mary asked.

Weeping, he said, "Nowhere . . . Bethany. . . . It's terrible. Everything's gone wrong. . . ."

"What's the matter that you so shamelessly weep in front of us?" Magdalene asked.

Sobbing uncontrollably, his words muddled, he said, "They condemned Jesus to death."

Horrified, the two women's confused minds numbed, while their bodies and souls instantly trembled in disbelief, fear, and denial. Tears spilled down their blanched cheeks. Loss, desolation, and emptiness overwhelmed their feelings, for their hearts had been crushed. The mother who bore Jesus would now witness his dying. The woman who loved him with the fullness of her transformed life would now behold him only in death. Without thinking, they grasped and held each other and wept in bitter sorrow for a long moment. Finally, they muttered, "No, no, please, it can't be."

"I'm sorry, I'm so sorry," John said, "but it is. . . ."

Magdalene asked, "What happened?"

"The Roman governor condemned him to death this morning."

Straining to calm herself, Mary asked, "Why did he do that, John?"

"The Sanhedrin found Jesus guilt of blasphemy. Jewish law claims it is an offense against God, punishable by death. But the Jews aren't allowed to impose such a sentence, only the Romans. So the Sanhedrin went to Pilate, the governor, and demanded he crucify Jesus."

At the word *crucify*, both women gasped.

"Oh my God, no," Mary said.

"Where are his friends?" Magdalene asked.

"I don't know—scattered. . . . I'm so ashamed. . . ."

"Were you fleeing, too?" Mary asked.

"Yes, I'm so sorry . . . I intended to go to Bethany to tell Lazarus and his sisters."

"That can wait. They'll learn soon enough," Magdalene said.

"Did all his friends abandon him?" Mary asked.

"Yes," John answered, his head slumping. "When they arrested Jesus we all fled."

"Well, John," Mary began, "now you have opportunity to redeem yourself. Take us to where Jesus is, and then stay with us to reveal the courage Jesus expects of you, even if you, too, are meant to die."

Bowing his head, John said, "Yes, I will, I will. . . ."

They crossed the arched bridge into the Upper City,

joining the throng of people trailing Jesus in his agonizing journey to Calvary. The dense crowd prevented them from getting close to Jesus. All walked slowly, a pace Jesus set, as he struggled to bear the weight of the cross beam on his sorrowful way to certain death. Behind Mary, Magdalene, and John, more people joined this somber multitude of Jerusalem's rich and poor. Soon the three were entirely surrounded by a slow-moving mass of Jerusalem's curious inhabitants who wanted to witness the gruesome deaths that an intimidated Roman governor so capriciously imposed upon both the guilty and an innocent.

CHAPTER 25

Dream and reality.

Claudia Procula, aristocratic wife of Pontius Pilate, dreamt an angry, unruly mob brought before her husband a silent, enigmatic man, demanding the governor condemn him to death. Pervasive within her dream was an overwhelming sense of the man's innocence, such that upon waking she was greatly troubled. She wondered why she would have such a disturbing dream until a loud, restless crowd gathered on the stone-paved courtyard of the Praetorium beneath Pilate's seat of judgment. When she saw Jesus, whom she had never encountered before, standing in front of her husband, she returned to her bed chamber and wrote him a note, pleading that he have nothing to do with that just man. She gave it to her servant girl with instruction not to return until Pilate had read Claudia's words.

Shouts of, "Crucify him, crucify him. . . ." echoed throughout Pilate's quarters in the opulent palace built by Herod the Great. In Claudia's mind she begged her husband not to be swayed by that cruel ultimatum, but she felt helpless. She could not interfere further. She could not go to him, entreating more. She had done all that Pilate would permit. What she feared and hated most was his weakness, allowing himself to be influenced by a hostile populace in matters that neither Rome nor Pilate cared about. One such matter was local religion; Rome encouraged her governors to be tolerant and accommodating. Thus, Pilate, in spite of his wife's earnest appeal, obliged the mob's demand and delivered Jesus up to them to be crucified.

"Why did you ignore my note?" she asked.

Greatly agitated, Pontius Pilate paced in front of his wife, now as annoyed with her question, as he was with the note itself. "Am I to let your dreams influence my conduct of the Empire's affairs?"

"No, I suppose not, but sparing the life of an innocent man surely couldn't alter the destiny of Rome."

"I am to assure the tranquility and order of this province. That is what Tiberius, the Senate, and your father expect of me and all governors. If it means sacrificing one lowly Nazarene trouble maker, then I have to do it."

"But you are the one who possesses power, Pontius, not the Jews," Claudia said.

"Rome respects local cultures and religions. You know that. In those matters I'm obliged to cater to these people."

"Why did they want him killed?"

"Because he blasphemed their God. Their religion claims that is a crime punishable by death."

"But you yourself found no cause in the man, no reason to kill him."

"Of course I found him innocent. I don't believe in the Jew's religion. I'm a Roman. I have my own gods."

"Then why did you allow him to be crucified?"

"Because I have to cater to the demands of the high priests and the Sanhedrin, regardless of my personal judgment. They came to me and claimed, very insistently, unless I put this man to death there would be a riot, possibly even rebellion. If that were to happen then I'm compelled to use my army to crush it, probably with many lives lost, both Roman and Jew. I had the opportunity to avoid that by granting their demand. Better that one man die than many. Surely you can agree with that."

"You have more than adequate military force in Jerusalem to prevent a riot. You could order a curfew, put soldiers on all the streets, threaten the high priests. They seem treacherous enough to incite a riot themselves. In other words, Pontius, use the power of Rome that you possess. Don't kill an innocent man just to appease an ugly mob and their blood-thirsty leaders."

"Well I can't change anything now. He's probably hanging on the cross already."

"How utterly barbaric of you to condemn a just man to such a death."

"Claudia, please. . . ."

"And you had him scourged. That was completely unnecessary. Why did you do that?"

"I thought it sufficient to annul their demands for crucifixion. I was wrong . . . a mistake on my part, but so what? He was destined to die anyway. That scourging? . . . soon forgotten."

"Not by me," Claudia said. "It was terribly cruel of you. I stood on the balcony above the courtyard. I saw your soldiers tie him to a pillar. I saw that brute of an animal whip Jesus nearly to death. I wept at the sight. And then do you know what happened?"

"No, what?"

"Jesus glanced upward and looked at me, looked into my eyes. I recognized his innocence, his goodness, his purity. It was then I knew you had done something evil."

"Don't talk foolishness. It would have been evil to release him. It would have caused a riot with many killed. That would have been evil."

"He looked at me in a way I had never known before, not even in the eyes of my lovers. It was as though he knew me, and knew I sent you that note, and that he even forgave you for ignoring it. But I saw his love for me. His were eyes of perfect love and forgiveness. I can't describe it any other way."

"You rant like a deceived woman. He was delirious with pain. His eyes revealed delirium not love."

"Tell me, Pontius, have you no feelings of remorse—no regret for sending him to his death?"

"None! First of all, I didn't send him to his death. The chief priests and elders did. I washed my hands of the whole affair. They killed Jesus, not me. I merely accommodated their demands, something Rome expects of me."

Claudia went to the balcony from where she had observed Jesus scourged. Below her a slave was already scrubbing away the blood of Jesus that would, left untended, permanently stain the stone floor. *How efficient my husband is,* she thought. *How quickly he erases evidence of his brutality.*

In the garden beyond the courtyard, light breezes whispered through the high palm branches, while the long rows of cypress, standing straight and still, shouted at Claudia Procula, "Remember Rome!"

Turning back toward Pilate she said, "There were times when I used to think I knew you so well."

"You know me better than anyone."

"I understood that on occasion you had to use deadly force to quell rebellion. I knew enemies of Rome were killed because of your commands. I'm a daughter of Rome. I know her ways. I know the empire must be preserved."

"Then why do you question my judgment now?"

"Because I learned something about you I had never known before. You are a cruel and brutal man, Pontius."

"I couldn't govern if I weren't cruel. No governor could. It's the only thing these provincials understand. But, wife, I've never been cruel to you."

"You dare not be. . . ."

Both knew that Claudia's father remained friends with influential members of the Roman Senate. Were Pilate ever to physically abuse his wife, he would be stripped of his rank and banished in exile.

"You are a man devoid of compassion and pity, with such a pathetic sense of justice that you allowed the most innocent of men to be put to death."

"How do you know he's innocent? You can't believe a silly dream."

"Yes, I do, more than ever. My eyes confirmed it."

"That's utter foolishness! Your dreams mean nothing! You get a thought in your head and you obsess. I made a decision, the right decision, a decision that you, as my wife and a Roman, are obliged to endorse. So say no more of it!"

"I'll say only this: I've lost respect for you. I cannot love a man I no longer respect."

"You didn't marry me for love. Your father had the ear of Tiberius; he promised to make me a governor and you a governor's wife. You wanted that as much as I did. I wonder sometimes if you ever loved me."

"That's not entirely true. You know I grew fond of you

in the early years, when we still lived in Rome, and our children were small. Was it love, I felt? Perhaps. . . ."

As a much younger man, Pilate came to love his wife and the two children she bore. Now, after years of a commonplace marriage in which she tried to please him more often than not, he still regarded her fondly. If that fondness no longer sustained the fervor of youth, it remained at least a genuine appreciation.

Nevertheless, he was now roused to anger and said, "As my wife, you have duties and responsibilities to honor. So long as I am governor and you are my wife, you will perform them . . . you will do as I say! And whether you love me or not, you will adorn my bed whenever I wish, just as you always have." Pilate turned and walked away.

Claudia Procula withdrew to her private chamber. From the high windows, she gazed over nearly the whole of Jerusalem, realizing she didn't want to be here ever again. She resented her husband forcing her to accompany him to a city she could never be comfortable in, with people who would never befriend her. She had come to enjoy living in the royal seaside palace at Caesarea with its warm sea breezes and her many Roman friends there. Even Pilate's temperament seemed more tolerable away from Jerusalem. But now she realized she would leave all of it behind. She decided to return to her true home on the river Tiber.

After a silent supper with Pontius, she said, "When we get back to Caesarea, I'm going to pack my things and take the first ship back to Rome."

"Why?" Pilate asked. "Do you need a little vacation? Do you want to see your parents?"

"Yes, I do," she said. "But that isn't my primary reason."

"What is it then?"

With irrevocable conviction, Claudia said, "I want a divorce."

CHAPTER 26

The death of Judas.

After kissing the cheek of Jesus to the approval and relief of Simon, Samuel, several lesser Temple priests, and a band of Jewish soldiers with torches and swords, young Judas Iscariot spent a restless, nearly sleepless night in the bed of a now familiar prostitute, his hand clenched around a fine purse that held thirty pieces of Roman silver. Only as the eastern sky slowly brightened, did Judas fall asleep.

On waking, the woman whose bed he shared was gone. Judas, his groin, buttock, and legs sticky and sweaty, needed to bathe, but he realized he'd have to do that later. Dressing hurriedly amid a stench of human waste and the odor of intercourse, all commixed with stale perfume, he felt a disgust and emptiness unlike anything he had ever experienced. He felt unclean in body, but also in another way, a way that disturbed him to the core of his being, for he realized these illicit acts that Jesus warned against had soiled his soul. Repulsed by feelings of his own raw immorality, Judas resolved, in spite of the ephemeral pleasures it offered, never to visit this house again. He thought of the young woman who tempted him, recognizing finally that she was to be pitied far more than the men who paid to use and abuse her.

He thought then of Jesus, of kissing him and being rewarded for it, though it provided no satisfaction, no pleasure, no hope, and no relief from horrid inner feelings of depravity.

He wondered what happened to Jesus after last seeing him cross over to the Upper City. *Did Jesus sleep in a palatial bed?* as Simon suggested. *And where was Jesus now?* If anything, Judas's thoughts intensified his spiritual despair and isolation.

The keeper of the house said, "Come again soon . . . you're always welcome here."

Judas looked at her and said, "No—I'm done with this house forever."

She smiled at the coarse, young Judean while thinking, *he'll be back.*

Stepping outside, Judas found the Old City nearly deserted. When he reached the Lower City, few children played in the streets and alleys, unlike other days. Market shoppers beneath the arched causeway were surprisingly sparse and that, in spite of hunger, made stealing bread and fruit too dangerous. With smaller coins he purchased food from the same merchants he had previously stolen from.

He ate on the steps of the Herodian Staircase before

ascending them. He wondered why the lower precincts were so devoid of activity, as was the Court of the Gentiles where he found Simon's stall vacant. Finally, he crossed to the Upper City, which also seemed unnaturally quiet.

A wretched-looking old man, an odd smile on his thin, gray lips, approached Judas who asked, "Where is everyone?"

"It's crucifixion day." The foul-smelling man grinned, showing his rotted teeth. "People enjoy a bloody spectacle every now and then."

"Oh, yes," Judas said, "two thieves crucified by the Romans. I knew that. I just forgot."

Smiling sardonically, the man replied, "Not two —three!"

"Three thieves. . . ." Judas laughed in relief at not being one of them.

"But one isn't a thief," the man said, mischievously.

A sudden confusion, or was it fear, seized Judas's mind. "Who's the third?"

"Why it's that Galilean trouble maker, Jesus of Nazareth. Pilate condemned that charlatan just this morning. The people demanded it, as did I," he said, with demoniac pride. "Where were you? It seemed like all of Jerusalem was there."

Horrified, Judas screamed, "No!" so loudly that it blemished the still, midday air and the heedless minds of the few who heard it.

With the old man behind, struggling to keep pace, Judas ran to reach the rear of a crowd that moved unhurriedly along narrow streets and steps leading to the hill of Calvary. Judas asked no one in particular, "Why is everyone walking so slowly?"

"We're following Jesus of Nazareth," someone replied.

"He carries the cross beam from which he will hang," another said. "He's already fallen twice."

"Well, I suppose we can't expect him to run," the old man said, laughing.

Facing him, a woman said, "Have you no respect for an innocent man about to be crucified?"

The old man sneered and limped away.

Around the base of the hill, Roman soldiers had established a perimeter of standing spears that the crowd pressed against. A Centurion stood guard at the path leading to where three men were being prepared for their agonizing deaths. Judas approached the Roman and asked, "Can I go to my friend Jesus?"

"Get out of here," the soldier replied. "Are you so stupid to think I'd let you anywhere near the condemned? Nobody gets close—not till they're all dead!"

Suddenly, from the top of the hill, everyone heard three men shrieking in unbearable pain.

"What's happening?" Judas asked.

"They're nailing their hands to the cross beam. Now get out of here, or go stand over there with the crowd."

Horror overwhelmed every aspect of Judas's being. He could not understand how Jesus came to be put to death. It was incomprehensible to him. *What could possibly have happened,* he wondered, *after he kissed Jesus in the Garden of Gethsemane? Did he not converse with Jerusalem's most important men?* as Simon had predicted.

Confused and troubled, Judas ran from the hill of crucifixion back to the city and Temple to confront Simon.

"But Judas, he *was* taken to converse with Jerusalem's most important men," Simon said. "Unfortunately, your Jesus refused to talk. He went from one important personage to another, refusing to answer their very legitimate questions about his life and teachings."

"Are you saying he's being crucified because he refused to answer questions?"

"No, not at all. When he was called before the Sanhedrin—I was there—your Jesus committed a grave offense against God. He blasphemed while being questioned by the Sanhedrin. And that, if you know our religion, is a sin punishable by death."

"Jesus would never blaspheme," Judas said. "He loves God. He calls God his father."

"Exactly, and therein lies the blasphemy. He declared himself the Son of God. I wish you could have seen our reactions. We were speechless, as we all knew that your Jesus had just willingly condemned himself to death by making that claim."

"I don't understand. You said he'd sleep in a palace, and today I'd be with him again. You lied to me. You betrayed me."

Simon laughed. "Betrayed you? Don't talk nonsense."

"Had I known this would happen, I never would have agreed to take you to him; I never would have kissed him."

"Judas, you either own a poor memory or are truly stupid. Have you forgotten our dinner conversation with Samuel? Have you forgotten that we have eye witnesses who would testify that you are a thief and murderer? Have you forgotten that had you not done what we asked, you would have been the one crucified today? So, tell me, who would you prefer to see crucified this afternoon, Jesus or yourself?"

Terrified by the question and knowing his only true answer, Judas was stunned into silence.

"I thought so," Simon said. "As grievous as your crimes are, the sin of Jesus is far greater."

"No," Judas replied. "It should have been me, not Jesus. He's innocent."

"You have no understanding of our religion. It had to be Jesus, even though you're a murderer and thief. Be grateful you're not hanging on a cross next to him."

Judas reached into his cloak's deep, inner pocket. "Here," he said, attempting to hand the purse with thirty Roman silvers to Simon. "This is blood money. I don't want it."

"But I didn't pay you," Simon said. "It was the Sanhedrin."

Turning from Simon, Judas rushed to the hall of the Sanhedrin where he encountered Samuel who asked, "What the hell are you doing here?"

"You and Simon tricked me into identifying Jesus, and then you had him murdered. You planned it."

"Guards," Samuel shouted.

Holding the money bag in his raised hand, Judas said, "This is blood money. For it you killed an innocent man." He threw the bag at Samuel's feet, silver pieces spilling onto the stone floor.

Two Temple guards grabbed Judas by the arms. Samuel said, "Throw that bum out of here!"

The guards dragged Judas away from Samuel, but Judas shouted again, "You killed an innocent man."

In a stronger, louder, resounding voice, Samuel shouted at Judas, "But you betrayed him with a kiss. You killed Jesus, not us!"

Filled with bitterness, and self-loathing, Judas wandered the empty streets of Jerusalem. Regret, confusion, disgust, and deep grief overwhelmed his thoughts and emotions. Having slept little the past two nights, he felt exhausted, although a wild, visceral raging within demanded he do something to somehow remove the horrid reality of his role in the crucifixion of Jesus.

In his heart a frantic battle raged between hurt and

hate: hurt he had endured ever since his sad boyhood and hate for those, indifferent and harsh, who still insulted him with the curse of stupidity. His dreams of working in this splendid capital, of marrying and fathering children, of owning a small, tidy house in the Lower City, no longer mattered. He scorned his Jerusalem dreams, knowing his most urgent obligation was to atone for the arrest, crucifixion, and death of Jesus.

He left the city through the Fish Gate in the northernmost wall. From a nearby hill he saw the distant hill of Calvary with its three crosses. He leaned against a large sycamore tree and wept for the dying Jesus, his tears distilled from the pure pain that years ago seared his boyhood heart. He wept as he hadn't since he was a frightened, lonely youth, ridiculed and rejected by the cruel, laughing boys of Kerioth. Their chant, *Stupid Judas, Stupid Judas, Stupid Judas,* pounded his brain. Now that never dormant, unhealed childhood wound surged into his distorted, despairing consciousness, merging with an unbearable sorrow he felt for initiating the events that led to the inevitable death of Jesus. This overpowering fusion of suffering provoked merely a single thought. He welcomed it, agreed to it, even rejoiced in it, for he knew it was what he must do to atone for his fatal kiss of Jesus.

Judas dried his eyes with his sleeve. He ran back to Jerusalem where he had passed a livery earlier. Entering, he found it deserted save for four horses in stalls at the rear of the stable. They whinnied and stomped at his unfamiliar presence. Judas glanced around, then spotted halters hanging on a wall. He suspected one would work, so he took it. Leaving, he noticed a horse, a mare, watching him, her gaze intent, ears perked, and wondering if this intruder was going to place the halter on her head. Judas read her mind, slightly amusing him.

But then something unrelated and astonishing, a realization he had thoughtlessly ignored, entered and stunned his entire being: Jesus, and Jesus alone, had always been kind to him.

What a fool I am, he thought, and in his deepest despair, *what a stupid fool!*

Without hesitation or reflection, he reached into his cloak and withdrew the fine water bag he had stolen from John. He hung it where the halter had hung, certain that it was as valuable. He looked at the mare still watching him and said out loud, "Never again will I steal. I am a thief no more."

A coming storm spawned high winds and a darkening sky. Judas rushed back to the lonely tree where he had wept. Gazing again at a gray, distant Calvary, though barely able to make out three crosses as the air thickened with dust and rain, he wondered if Jesus had already died. He sobbed uncontrollably at the realization of Jesus crucified.

Finally, gaining control of himself, he placed the halter's noseband over his head and around his neck. He climbed the tree to stand on a large, nearly horizontal branch. At the level of his chin, he grabbed and hung from a sturdy stump of a branch, higher than his height above the ground. The stump held Judas's full weight. He turned his back against the trunk, slipping the crownpiece of the halter over the stump. Now all that remained for young Judas Iscariot was mustering the will to jump off the branch. He knew he would be choked to death. He accepted it. It was the only atonement presented to him, for in his self-loathing he could think of no other. Then, filled with far more remorse than self-pity, he stepped off the branch. His body dropped less than the length of a horse's head. The strong, leather, noseband strangled him like a murderer's hands, forcing his tongue to project grotesquely out from the side of his mouth. With legs flailing wildly, instinct compelled him to grasp for the strap, but his fingers could not squeeze between it and his neck. In a moment, Judas's arms dropped limply to his side. His legs went straight and still. His dying body, swaying slightly in the wind, sagged earthward, while his last conscious thought begged Jesus to forgive.

EPILOGUE

A final prophecy.

Two women and a young man stood amidst a crowd of curious on-lookers at the base of a rocky hill, unable to approach three crucified criminals, simply because the Roman soldiers did not allow it. After the crosses were raised, the screams of the suffering men were easily heard, but as the seconds and minutes of the afternoon slowly passed, and as the men's weakened bodies gradually descended toward death, their screams became barely audible groans of intense agony. Two thieves on either side of the man in the center could be seen wagging their heads in a vain attempt to ease in the slightest their torture. However, the man hanging on the center cross did not move similarly only because to do so would disturb deep puncture wounds in his scalp, inflicted by a crown of thorns mockingly thrust onto his head.

Death by crucifixion consumed time, its suffering prolonged until the crucified could no longer even raise their heads. The groaning, too, ended. As death drew nearer the three, the crowd began to disperse. Dark clouds, distant in the morning west, now covered the whole of Judea, prompting more of the crowd to abandon the desolate hill. A Roman Centurion, the same one who turned Judas away several hours earlier, dismissed those soldiers who had accomplished the brutal work. He remained, however, to guard the path leading to a small plateau where the crucified were dying. Finally, only three persons lingered. They stared intently at the man on the center cross until the young man put his arms around the women's shoulders, urging them toward the Centurion.

"Can we approach the crosses now?" the young man asked.

"Who are you?" the Centurion replied.

"My name is John. I'm a friend of the man on the center cross."

"Oh, the King of the Jews. . . ."

"No," the older woman said. "His name is Jesus."

"And who are you?"

"I am his mother; my name is Mary. I come from Nazareth."

A suffocating sorrow had settled into Mary's heart where only yesterday a joyous expectation resided. With happiness she had anticipated celebrating Passover with Jesus and his friends, but that sweet prospect had been utterly destroyed by a series and sequence of events and circumstances that she could never have imagined. Now she knew her earthly fate: from his first stirrings in her womb to his final breath on the cross, she, and she alone, beheld the full arc of his simple yet remarkable life; a life that changed so many hearts and minds, as he wandered along the shores and amid the hills and towns of Palestine. Thousands heard, accepted, and followed his radical teachings of love and forgiveness. He had become a leader in the religious lives of so many that Jerusalem's most powerful men feared him to the point where only his death could restore their comfort and their claims.

Jesus was a nuisance, a detractor, one who challenged the authority of ancient ways, but claimed to fulfill the prophetic vision of a suffering servant with the simple teaching that men and women are to love one another, as they love themselves. Above all, they were to know that God was their Father who created and loved them. They were to adore him, not by animal sacrifices, petty, repetitious laws, or mindless rote prayer, but with compassionate hearts for the least of those among them.

"And who is this other woman?"

"I am Magdalene from the town of Capernaum in the north. I, too, am a friend of Jesus."

"Well, unfortunately, I can't let you get any closer. My orders don't allow it."

"Sir," John said, "I don't see any other Roman soldiers here. Is your superior officer here?"

"No, they've all left."

"Couldn't we then approach our friend, to be with him while he's dying?"

"Look, I have my orders. Do you really think I'd disobey because my superior isn't here?"

"No, of course not," Mary said. "We understand."

"Besides, crucifixion is too gruesome. You women shouldn't see it up close. It's a cruel, terrible punishment. Spare yourself the horror of witnessing your son dying in agony."

"Tell me," John said, trying to shift the Centurion's thinking, "what did you hear people say about our friend Jesus?"

"Some said he was a prophet; others said he was a man of God; most said he was innocent, unjustly condemned. A few said he was a false prophet. One old fellow"—the same foul-smelling creature Judas encountered earlier—"even yelled if Jesus was a man of God, a true prophet, someone who saved others, then he should save himself and come down from the cross. Can you imagine that? I assure you, there's no way anyone, prophet or not, could save himself from a Roman crucifixion."

The wind strengthened, as skies continued to darken. The milling crowd had left the wretched spectacle and returned to their homes in preparation for Passover.

Mary said, "Sir, I beg of you, leave your post now since all the others have gone. Go to your barrack. Then you do not disobey your orders. If you are not here, we climb the hill at our own peril."

"No, I will not abandon my post. Don't forget lady, I'm a Centurion!" He said it with great pride. "Besides, I have to stay here until they're all dead. In fact, I have to make sure they *are* dead."

"We have a Centurion in our town," Magdalene said to distract. "He's a very fine man and a friend of Jesus."

He was surprised to hear it. "Well, I never met your Jesus, but I consider myself a fine man, too, as does my wife."

"I'm sure you are," Magdalene said.

"Then I beg you," Mary said again, "let us be with my son as he dies. Please, I beg you. Let us pass."

The Centurion thought for several moments. He saw Mary's glistening eyes catch the dimming light, and Magdalene's. Then they all heard a loud, anguished voice cry out.

"That's the voice of Jesus," Mary said, softly weeping. "Sir, please let us pass. I beg you."

"What did he say?"

"All I understood was 'My God, my God. . . .'4"

He gazed into Mary's beseeching eyes. "I shouldn't do this," he paused, "but alright, go ahead."

Mary, John, and Magdalen thanked the Centurion with fervent sincerity, something he wasn't used to. "Hey, Mother Mary," he called, "what makes your son, Jesus, so special?"

---

4 Matthew 27:46, Mark 15:34

Her heart broken yet filled with faith in the words of the ancient prophets, Mary turned and said, "You will see . . . in time you will see."

The End.

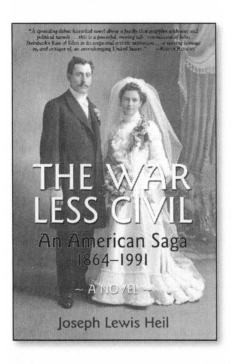

Made in the USA
Middletown, DE
20 February 2022

61584741R00111